TROUBLE ON THE TRAIL

Fargo heard war cries and galloping hooves behind him. He spun, keeping low, making as small a target of himself as possible. He holstered the Colt and brought the Henry into firing position, chambering another round.

Two Apaches were riding their ponies at him, hell-bent for leather, from separate directions. They were whooping it up and each held a lance decorated with tribal war feathers. Sharpened steel points glinted murderously in the sunshine.

The Henry roared. Fargo rode the recoil.

The Apache to his left was knocked from the saddle, as if jerked by an invisible rope. He hit the ground and did not move.

The other horseman stormed directly at him, the on-coming lance aimed at Fargo's body. He fired but the Apache saw it coming and leaned sideways atop his mount without slowing. What should have been a head shot missed completely.

Then the horseman was upon him.

THE TRAILSMAN
#250

ARIZONA AMBUSH

by

Jon Sharpe

A SIGNET BOOK

SIGNET
Published by New American Library, a division of
Penguin Putnam Inc., 375 Hudson Street,
New York, New York 10014, U.S.A.
Penguin Books Ltd, 80 Strand,
London WC2R 0RL, England
Penguin Books Australia Ltd, Ringwood,
Victoria, Australia
Penguin Books Canada Ltd, 10 Alcorn Avenue,
Toronto, Ontario, Canada M4V 3B2
Penguin Books (N.Z.) Ltd, 182–190 Wairau Road,
Auckland 10, New Zealand

Penguin Books Ltd, Registered Offices:
Harmondsworth, Middlesex, England

First published by Signet, an imprint of New American Library,
a division of Penguin Putnam Inc.

First Printing, August 2002
10 9 8 7 6 5 4 3 2 1

The Trailsman

Beginnings . . . they bend the tree and they mark the man. Skye Fargo was born when he was eighteen. Terror was his midwife, vengeance his first cry. Killing spawned Skye Fargo, ruthless, cold-blooded murder. Out of the acrid smoke of gunpowder still hanging in the air, he rose, cried out a promise never forgotten.

The Trailsman they began to call him all across the West: searcher, scout, hunter, the man who could see where others only looked, his skills for hire but not his soul, the man who lived each day to the fullest, yet trailed each tomorrow. Skye Fargo, the Trailsman, the seeker who could take the wildness of a land and the wanting of a woman and make them his own.

Arizona Territory, 1860—
Where a woman's will is not always her own,
and the best things in life go to the men
willing to take them.

1

She looked like trouble.

Luckily for Skye Fargo, she looked like the kind of trouble he didn't mind getting into . . . in more ways than one.

"Buy a girl a drink, handsome?"

She was maybe twenty, probably younger. Her figure, encased in a dance hall getup, curved in all of the right places.

The tall man in buckskins, known as the Trailsman, was leaning against the bar of a place called The Bucket of Blood in Quartz, Arizona Territory, nursing a lukewarm beer that tasted like champagne, the way it cut through the trail dust that parched his throat.

"Why sure, ma'am," he grinned. "What's your pleasure?"

She turned to the hovering bartender and ordered for herself. "The usual, Dave."

The mustached barkeep sauntered off.

Fargo was willing to bet that "the usual" was a shotglass of water with a drop of brown food coloring to make it look like whiskey. Fargo was no stranger to trail town honky-tonks like this one and the women who worked the riders passing through. He understood the rules of the game and was willing to play by those rules when the trail got lonesome.

Dusk was graying the windows of the barroom. Despite the fact that the bar was half full and rang to the laughter of men and some women, as well as to the tune of a player piano, Fargo felt that particular, aching loneliness of the trail that only a woman could cure.

The bartender brought the "shot" to the curvy redhead. Fargo paid him, and clinked glasses with her.

She smiled sweetly. "To new acquaintances."

As they sipped their drinks, Fargo's seasoned eyes openly assessed her. At no more than a hundred pounds, her height was a foot less than his. She was a cute little morsel. Curly red hair fell around a pretty, freckled Irish face of peaches-and-cream complexion, pouty red lips, and sparkling green eyes. The slightest layer of baby fat, and innocence in those vivacious eyes, only heightened the erotic effect of her lush young breasts pushed up and almost out of her plunging neckline.

And it was that sense of innocence that bothered Fargo, as did the circle of white around the fourth finger of her left hand. A wedding band had graced that finger until not very long ago.

But he was not a man to turn down an inviting smile from a beautiful woman. And the ride in from Yuma had been long and hard. He'd delivered the prisoner from Tucson to the prison as the territory, which depended on contract freelancers like himself for much of what little law enforcement there was in these parts, had hired him to. The prisoner had been convicted of killing a miner, as well as his wife and daughter, to gain hold of their claim and had tried to escape three times while in Fargo's custody. It had not been an easy job, and he was on his way back to Colorado where the weather suited him better this time of year. But the two-day ride thus far from Yuma had been brutally hot and dusty.

"What's your name, darlin'?" he asked this redheaded cutie.

Her smile was dimpled and cute as hell, but he could read human emotion as well as he could read sign on the trail, and Fargo detected a hesitation within her, as if she were an actress still learning her lines.

"You can call me Desiree."

"Well, howdy, Desiree. You can call me Skye."

"Pleased to make your acquaintance." She finished the contents of her shotglass. "Buy me another?"

"I reckon." As he lifted an arm to summon the bartender, he added, "You're a mite young to be working in a place like this, aren't you, Desiree?"

Skye, you're a fool, he was telling himself. *Here you've got the sweetest little piece of goods you've seen in a long time, serving herself up to you for the price of a few drinks, and your damn conscience wants to get in the way . . .*

Desiree swallowed a quick gulp from the shotglass Dave brought her. "I'm old enough to know what I'm doing."

Fargo chuckled, taking another sip of his half-full beer that was becoming warmer by the second.

"Simmer down. I wouldn't be talking to you at all if I didn't think you were a grown woman who can make her own choices."

She blinked prettily, looking somewhat taken aback. "Well, thank you for that, at least."

"It's just that I can tell you're new at this," he added in a friendly tone. "I want you to do well in your new line of endeavor."

She looked flustered, standing there at the bar in her low-cut outfit. "You're making fun of me. That's not nice. And what makes you think this is a new line of endeavor?" she asked tartly.

"You don't want to use that tone," he advised. "You want to be polite to the boys who ride through looking for a night of female companionship. If they're looking for a thin-skinned shrew, they'll wait until they get back home to their wives or girlfriends."

She bristled. "Thin-skinned shrew? What makes you think—"

From behind them, a voice shouted, "Emma!"

Sudden silence descended upon the smoky barroom. Everyone made way for the man who had stomped in and now stood just inside, the bat-wing doors swinging behind him. Someone kicked the player piano and it stopped tinkering away.

The young man wore the coveralls and straw hat of a farmer. He wasn't armed, but his fists were clenched and his eyes were centered on the woman who stood next to Fargo. He stormed forward.

She whirled to face him. "Jed! What are you doing here?"

"I should ask you that question," he said in a firm, measured voice. He grabbed her by a wrist. "You're coming home with me, Emma. What the devil do you think you're doing in a place like this?" He stared around with disgust. "Why did you leave me, honey? I've been a day getting here. My God, I hope you haven't—" He couldn't complete the sentence.

"No, I haven't, Jed," she assured him in a peculiarly gentle voice that Fargo hadn't heard her use before. "Today is my first day, honest. I just started."

"Emma—"

"Jed, I swear that's the truth." She indicated Fargo. "This is the first gentleman who's bought me a drink. You never listen to me, Jed. You're always too busy with the crops and the figures in the ledger book. It's you who drove me away."

Jed didn't seem to hear her. And he didn't release his grip on her wrist. His glare swung to Fargo, utterly unimpressed by either the Trailsman's formidable size or by the formidable Colt holstered at Fargo's hip.

"So you thought you'd molest my wife, is that it, stranger?"

Oh hell, Fargo thought. He spoke in a reasonable voice. "First things first, friend."

"I ain't your friend."

"Whatever you say, Jed. Now unhand the lady."

"You watch your mouth, mister. This here's my wife. We're in love with each other, Emma and me. Ain't that so, honey?"

Her eyes lowered. "I do love you, Jed," she admitted. "But sometimes I don't know if you love me, or if you just think you own me. I thought I had to get away," she concluded in a choked voice, "but I . . . I don't know what I think."

4

"We've got ourselves a good home, a little farm a mile out of town," Jed told Fargo. "Until Emma went crazy day before last, that is. I'm here to bring her home."

"You're doing the right thing, Jed," said Fargo. "But you're doing it the wrong way." He nodded at the young man's white-knuckled hand that held her wrist like a vise. "Let her go, friend. Don't make me ask you again."

There was hesitation. Jed looked into Fargo's eyes, and what he saw there made the farmer release his wife's wrist. But he glared at Fargo defiantly. "You oughta butt out and mind your own business."

Emma-Desiree massaged her sore wrist. She glanced in Fargo's direction, gratitude in her green eyes. "Thanks, mister. I'm sorry about this, really. I didn't know Jed was so, well, so hot-tempered."

"You go home with him," said Fargo. "Go back home and put on your wedding ring. You two have found love and that's something that seems to be in mighty short supply in this world." He indicated the smoky environ-ment of the barroom. "This is my world, not yours. Give him another chance, Emma. I reckon he'll try a mite harder to understand. Right, Jed?"

Jed nodded eagerly, not sure what to make of the stranger but certain that they were in total agreement. "You listen to the man, honey. It won't be like it was before, I promise. I didn't know I'd miss you so much."

There was a moment of hesitation before she lifted her head, drew her shapely figure erect and spoke to him eye to eye. "All right, Jed. I'll try it with you again. This was a big mistake. Let's go home."

As they walked toward the bat-wing doors, Jed threw a backward glance over his shoulder in Fargo's direction. "Much obliged, mister."

Fargo acknowledged this with an index finger tip of farewell from the brim of his hat. "Good luck to you, sodbuster."

Emma-Desiree also sent him a look over her shoulder during that final instant before the little redhead and her husband disappeared from sight. It was a glance that Jed did not see.

Fargo was unable to read the look across the distance of the barroom, and he wasn't sure if anyone else saw it. He adored women but, like most men he knew, he barely understood them at the best of times.

Within heartbeats of the couple leaving, the player piano resumed its merry tinkling and the laughter and raucous rabble of the honky-tonk returned.

That was fine with Fargo. Feeling relaxed, surrounded by the sounds of the bustling barroom around him, he turned back to the bar and finished his beer.

He became aware of a man standing next to him, a leathery-faced gent in his late fifties, stocky of build, wearing a duster over trousers, white shirt, and a jacket that bespoke financial success.

"Mr. Skye Fargo, I presume?" The man shouted to be heard above the barroom rabble.

"Maybe," said Fargo, squinting. "Do I know you?"

"Not yet, but you'll want to."

"You sound mighty sure of yourself, mister. Why is that?"

"Because I have two things to offer you, which, if your reputation is accurate, you value more than anything in the world."

Fargo regarded the man with mingled skepticism and amusement. "And what might those things be?"

The man chuckled confidently. "Money and adventure," he said. "I can offer you an abundance of both, Mr. Fargo. I have a most intriguing story to tell you. I think it best if we find a table. May I buy you a drink?"

2

"Is that or is that not," asked G.B. Mandell a few minutes later, "the prettiest young lady you ever did see?"

He and Fargo had found a scarred wooden table, located in a corner across the room from the player piano.

Couples had started dancing. An argument broke out at one of the poker tables. No one paid any attention to the two men who had withdrawn for their private conversation.

Mandell had set a carefully preserved photograph down on the table for Fargo's inspection. He leaned back in his chair and sipped his whiskey, awaiting Fargo's response. He'd shed his duster, and Fargo's initial impression of the man's prosperity was confirmed. Mr. G.B. Mandell, of Silver City, according to the card he'd presented Fargo, was easily the best-dressed gent in the place.

Fargo took a sip of the beer Mandell had bought him. It was no less lukewarm than his first. He stared down at the photograph, seeing the image of a young woman in her twenties, a lovely, Nordic face of high cheekbones, sensuous lips, and dazzling eyes that seemed to glow even from the flatness of the daguerreotype. Her nose was perhaps more pronounced than this beauty would have liked, thought Fargo, and her chin had a determined thrust with a slight cleft. But these only served to emphasize an impression of strength melded with sensuality. She reminded Fargo of a picture he'd seen once of some mythological Viking goddess. Her long blond hair was

7

severely braided onto either shoulder, but that hair would frame her sensuous face when it was let down and was tangled and damp from making love.

Fargo realized that he was being spoken to. He snapped his eyes up from the beauty in the picture, focusing his wandering mind.

"So as you well can imagine, Mr. Fargo," Mandell was saying . . . "any man would be outraged if his mail-order bride were kidnapped. But to lose a beauty such as Britt after only having known her for five short days . . ." He sighed heavily. He picked up the photograph gingerly, as if he were fondling the woman herself. He returned the photograph to an envelope and carefully replaced that in an inside jacket pocket. "I will pay you handsomely, sir, to rescue my wife-to-be from the brutes who have abducted her."

Mandell's card had stated that he was president of the Mandell Mining Works of Silver City. If the card were intended to get Fargo's attention, the ploy had succeeded. Mandell was amiable enough, gruff and authoritarian, but a man's man who was only slightly over the hill and seemed to know it.

Fargo said, "So you didn't actually marry the young lady."

Another massive sigh from Mandell. "We were to have been married today, actually. A week after she arrived. I am, well, as you can imagine, Mr. Fargo, I am a man of some, uh, prestige in Silver City. A degree of propriety had to be observed, of course."

"Of course." Fargo had never quite understood the notion of ordering a bride through the mail, but it was a common enough way for women in the Old World to find a passage to the New World, and for men like Mandell to find female companionship. "How much do you know about this girl?" he asked.

"The service I employed screens young ladies from only the best families," Mandell assured him. "Miss Lundgren's father ran a highly successful general store but fell upon hard times."

Fargo sipped his beer and winced. It was going from lukewarm to hot.

"It happens," he conceded.

"Additionally, my late wife, God rest her soul, was a prominent member of the social world in Silver City. Therefore, my remarriage is a matter of profound social interest there, if I may say so."

"How did you and Britt get along during those, what, five days?"

"Five days exactly. Why, we got along fine. She is a young woman of class and breeding, with a gift for laughter and parlor games such as I have never seen." Mandell's lips crinkled with a bitter smile. "All of my friends adored her, and she seemed most affectionate of me. She had already taken to fetching my slippers in the evening and fluffing the pillow of my reading chair."

"When did you get the ransom note?"

"An hour after I found her gone." Mandell produced a handkerchief and swabbed at his sweaty forehead. "I was able to raise the cash by the next morning. Five thousand dollars they wanted."

"You paid the ransom, and no Britt."

"Precisely." Mandell wadded the handkerchief into a ball and angrily thumped the table with his fist. "And I know who did it! They still have her! They were seen leaving town together, her and the two who held her captive. Silver City isn't that large a town. I did some asking around, and I've checked my connections every step of the way from there to here. I've been on their trail, you see. Their names are Taggart and Linder, and they're rumored to be fast with their guns. That's why I won't go after them myself, sir. I'm a businessman, not a shootist."

"Never heard of them."

"But you could find them if I paid you?"

"I can find anybody," said Fargo. He wasn't bragging, simply stating the truth.

"I have friends in high places in the territorial government," said Mandell. "I telegraphed them and they recommended you for the job. I tracked you here and I wasn't disappointed at what I just witnessed. I mean, the way you handled that young farmer and his wife. You displayed supreme self-discipline, sir, coupled with sound judgment. And I've heard of your exploits, of course. Who hasn't heard of the Trailsman? Yes, you are exactly the man I'm looking for."

"And what sort of job are you offering me?"

"I want Taggart and Linder tracked down and killed." Mandell leaned forward, an elbow upon the table. He lowered his voice. "I want them dead, and I want Britt brought back to me. I've paid good money for her passage to this country from Denmark, and I paid those bastards their ransom. They won't get anther nickel out of me. I want them dead, Fargo, and I'll pay you a thousand dollars to see that the job gets done right. Half now, half when Britt and I are reunited."

Fargo cleared his throat. "Uh, I'm sure you've considered the possibility that she left voluntarily with Taggart and Linder. Maybe she doesn't want to come home. Maybe she likes being an outlaw's woman."

Mandell's expression darkened. "Of course I've considered that possibility. But dammit, Fargo, that woman is going to be my wife! I'll not be made a fool of in my community, and it just so happens that I came to fall in love with Britt during those wonderful five days that we did spend together."

Fargo recalled the vibrancy that had emanated from the photograph of the Nordic goddess.

"I can see where that could happen," he said.

"If that is the case," said Mandell, "I mean if Britt is feeling as you say, well then, sir, I shall cross that bridge when I must. As for now, do you want the job or not?"

Of course he took the job.

A thousand dollars would go a long way toward that stretch of the good life he was looking forward to in Colorado. And besides, the job of tracking down Taggart and Linder was tailor-made for a man of his talents. But there was one condition: Fargo would turn the two kid-

10

nappers in to the local sheriff. He was, after all, the Trailsman, and not a hired assassin.

Fargo promised to stay in touch with Mandell, and ten minutes later he was at the livery stable, reclaiming his horse. In his pocket was the folded packet of greenbacks that the mining magnate had slipped to him under the table back in the saloon. Fargo's Henry repeating rifle was in its scabbard, he had a full canteen, and his impressive Ovaro stallion, a tall black-and-white paint with distinctive markings, had been fed and rested.

He'd ridden into this ramshackle little hamlet looking for an evening's lodging and hopefully some female companionship, true. But that was before G.B. Mandell came along. The way Fargo figured it, the sooner he earned the other half of his retainer, the sooner he could continue on to the piney coolness and the warm-blooded gals in the high country. So right now, his only concern was tracking down and dealing with a pair of hardcases named Taggart and Linder, and a missing bride-to-be named Britt.

He was cinching the saddle around the Ovaro's belly when he detected the slightest stir behind him. Fargo whirled, assuming a crouch, his Colt coming up lightning fast, the revolver aiming at the source of the slight sound.

"Step forward," he instructed.

The figure that materialized surprised him, as did the way she quickly crossed to him.

It was Emma-Desiree. She had changed into the plain, formless attire of a farmer's wife, but her curly red hair still framed the peaches-and-cream, youthful beauty that now glinted with mischief and something else.

That something else was lust, Fargo decided.

Even surrounded as they were by the earthy smells of the livery stable, there was a musky natural, arousing scent to her that mingled with the cheap perfume that still clung to her despite her change to respectable attire.

"I . . . I hope I didn't surprise you, Skye," she said in a breathy voice. Her complexion was flushed. She licked her pouty lips. They glistened in the warm light of the kerosene lamp.

He looked around. They were alone. He holstered his pistol.

"Women are always surprising me," he growled. "I've got to admit, ma'am, I didn't expect you. Uh, does your husband know you're here?"

"Of course not." Then suddenly she was against him, the contours of her firm young breasts and hips pressing into him. Her wrists joined at the back of his neck. Close up, he saw fires dancing in her green eyes. "Jed is a practical man. He had the horses fitted for shoes at the blacksmith since he was coming to town, you see. He's paying the smithy now so we can't be long."

She raised her lips to his and before he knew it, they were kissing.

What the hell, he decided. He drew her to him.

Her tongue slithered into his mouth like a succulent, hot snake. One of her hands slid down and cupped the front of his britches. Her warm hand slid around the shaft of his manhood through the material and she gave a knowing squeeze that made him grow hard.

"Uh, lady," he managed to say when their kiss ended, "are you sure this is such a great idea? I mean, I'm willing enough and all—"

"I can feel how willing you are." She raised herself onto her tiptoes and whispered into his ear, continuing to stroke him. "I'm taking your advice. I'm going back to my boring farmer husband to be a good little wife, like you said. Isn't that enough? But before I do, big man, I want me at least a taste of the wild life."

Then she somehow managed to slide an ankle behind one of his and, because his attention was on what she was doing to the front of his britches, she dropped him into the hay. The petite redhead tossed herself atop him, locking her lips to his and delivering another passionate, lewd kiss, her hips grinding against his.

Fargo gripped her nicely rounded bottom and effortlessly rolled the little tigress over onto her back.

Then a familiar voice shouted from behind them.

"Emma!"

The hard-breathing redhead stopped her passionate

writhing beneath Fargo, looking over his shoulder. "Oh drat!" she said. Then she was on her feet, backing away from Fargo. "Jed, honey, I didn't know what I was doing! He made me come in here with him!"

Jed's young face was as flushed as hers, but with rage, not lust. He stood in the doorway of the table, glaring at Fargo.

"Don't you worry none, honey," he snarled as he stormed forward. "I'll take care of this no-good snake, so's he'll never molest a good woman again!" He grabbed a nearby pitchfork without slowing and charged at Fargo like the pitchfork was a spear.

Fargo came to his feet, unwilling to draw a weapon on the outraged husband of a woman he'd had no business dallying with in the first place. On the other hand, he couldn't very well let this youngblood poke him full of holes. He waited until the charging farmer was upon him, then easily deflected the amateurishly aimed pitchfork, ripping it from Jed's grip with a sideways swipe. At the same time he brought the young man down with a clipped chop. Fargo unholstered his Colt and lowered a knee onto the heaving chest of the farmer, who was prone upon his back. Fargo touched the barrel of his Colt lengthwise along the side of the young man's head. The touch of its cool steel had an instantly calming effect on Jed. He stared up uncertainly at the man crouched above him.

Fargo said, "Just two things for you to ponder, son, when you wake up."

Jed's Adam's apple bobbed madly. His eyes widened. "Mister, wait! Don't do nothin' crazy!"

"One," said Fargo quietly, as if he hadn't been interrupted. "Maybe this little hot-britches gal you're married to ain't worth the trouble, sodbuster. And two, don't ever come at me with a pitchfork."

He rapped Jed with the barrel of the Colt hard enough to render the young man unconscious. Jed's snoring filled the stable.

Fargo stood and turned to face the woman who had watched everything from where she stood next to the wall. Her eyes shined more fiery than before. The bosom of her shapeless clothing heaved. She stepped forward.

"Skye, before you leave . . . my God, you're so masterful, the way you handled Jed. I *must* know a man like you at least once in my life! Please, Skye—"

She was almost upon him again when he swung into the saddle, towering over her.

"You'll excuse me, ma'am, but I've got a job to do. There are only two things that could make me stay. Love and money. Well, I've got the money. And darlin', I don't think you know a thing about love. But good luck to you anyway."

He tipped his hat to her and reined the stallion clear.

Then he was galloping out of Quartz, Arizona Territory, his horse's hooves carrying him back into the star-studded desert night.

Fargo found himself wondering which was more difficult, finding a woman to marry, as in G.B. Mandell's case, or keeping her satisfied once you found her, as in Jed's case.

He had been truthful when telling his new employer that he'd never heard the names of the hardcases, Taggart and Linder. But he did have a few ideas . . .

The meager lights of the town receded behind him.

3

It was dawn when Fargo reined in the Ovaro on a ridge
overlooking a stand of cottonwood trees along a winding
river that shone like a luminescent ribbon in the silvery
half-light of a new day.

Fargo had found what he was looking for.

It was an idyllic scene. Five Conestoga wagons had
been drawn into a half-circle around the trees. Smoke
from a cooking fire snaked skyward. Figures could be
seen, moving about. Some were bathing in the river. The
mule teams munched contentedly at tall sweetgrass
nearby.

Although he could discern no physical details from this
distance, one thing was apparent to Fargo: There were
only women down there. There was no sign of any men.

Fargo grinned to himself, "Lady Jay, you've been
found."

A slight pressure from his knees sent the Ovaro into
a canter down an incline, off the ridge through the scrub
brush, toward the small wagon train.

As the land leveled and he approached the wagons,
he lost sight of the women he had seen moving about.

But they would hear his horse's hooves. Sound carried
easily in the quiet dawn on these wide open spaces. And
so they would certainly have heard him. In fact, he was
making a point of not catching them by surprise.

He'd been riding all night. As far back as Tucson, a
day before he had encountered G.B. Mandell last night,
Fargo had heard talk, having eavesdropped on some

cowboys, about Lacy Jay's roaming bordello being in the territory, working the remote communities and ranches along the San Pedro. He had not joined in on the conversation, but had filed the information away. There had been a time when he and Lacy Jay had been lovers, and it had *not* been professional . . .

Her presence in the territory had re-entered his mind after he accepted Mandell's proposal and started thinking of leads to start tracking down the kidnapped mail-order bride.

Lacy Jay's cathouse-on-wheels was not unique. On the frontier, female companionship was scarce. There were those women who moved west with their husbands. There were women of pure virtue, schoolmarms and restaurant workers, mostly. And there were the whores.

Most towns had a motley collection of prostitutes working their cribs upstairs over a saloon or in shanties outside of town. Equally common were enterprising, traveling purveyors of the world's oldest profession. Lacy Jay brought the goods to lonesome trail herders and miners who had the money to spend and the itch for a woman, but could not afford to take time off for a two-day round-trip ride to the nearest town.

The difference between Lacy Jay's operation and those of her competitors was that her word-of-mouth advertising was the gospel truth: Lacy Jay really did have the prettiest and most talented whores working the circuit.

Cowboys were known to save two months' wages in anticipation of a rumored visit to the area by Lacy and her girls.

Fargo had reached the river hours ago, a few miles upstream. He followed the river south, keeping far enough in so that he would not reveal his presence. He passed one settlement, the male population of which was no doubt the reason Lacy Jay's wagon train had spent a week encamped under the stand of cottonwoods near town, thought Fargo. He'd also passed a sawmill and a ferry crossing before he found what he was looking for.

He was about twenty yards from the blind side of a

Conestoga wagon when a rifleshot rang out. He saw the spit of saffron flame, a muzzle flash from the side of the wagon, followed an instant later by a bullet ricocheting off a nearby boulder.

His horse quivered with surprise and reared back, pawing the air.

Fargo spoke reassuringly to the beast. He gripped the reins with one hand, fighting down his inclination to draw his Colt. The horse steadied itself.

Fargo dropped the reins. He lifted both arms to show the invisible shooter that he was empty-handed. "Whoa there, hair-trigger," he called. Despite the fact that the rifle report was still echoing on the air, he made his voice sound cordial. "A little early in the day for target practice, isn't it? I just rode out for a friendly visit."

"Well cowboy," came a tart female reply, "you rode out a day too late. Miss Lacy has us breaking camp and moving on directly after breakfast. She wants us to separate some soldier boys from their wages come payday this week up at Fort Grant. We been here for a week. Ain't you heard we was leaving?"

"I'm not here for that kind of a visit," he called back to her. "Would you kindly tell your Miss Lacy that Skye Fargo has come calling and would like an audience with the queen? That is, if she's not otherwise engaged."

There followed a long silence from the direction of the wagon. Then the girl said, "That's a mighty big mouthful for a gal to remember, stranger. But I will tell her that there's a good lookin' feller in buckskin that rode in and wants to see her. Will that do?"

Fargo lowered his hands. "That'll do fine. Thank you, sweetheart."

"But don't go getting no fancy ideas about getting in here," she cautioned in a voice that was hard beyond what looked like her tender years. "Miss Lacy, she keeps this here wagon train tighter than an army camp—except, of course, during working hours."

Fargo chuckled. "Yeah, sounds like Lacy hasn't changed much."

"You know Lacy?" the voice asked with genuine interest. "You know her from the old days, then. I don't recognize you."

"Yeah, it's been a while," said Fargo diplomatically. "And I've rode a mite to get here. Will you fetch her for me now?"

"I'll tell her you're here. But like I said, mister, don't get no fancy ideas. I got another girl right here and she's keeping this her rifle pointed at your gizzard."

"Right," said Fargo, knowing she was lying.

He waited fifteen seconds or so before nudging the Ovaro forward. The clumping of his horse's hooves had prevented him from hearing a rifle being cocked before the girl had fired, but he would hear any such sound at the lazy walk with which the horse now carried him. If there really were more rifle-toting prostitutes Fargo had enough faith in his instincts to know that he would see or sense their presence. In his estimation, the whore was bluffing about there being another girl drawing a bead on him. She'd only wanted to hold him at bay while she left her post.

He angled his horse between the wagons and entered the encampment in the clearing.

It was quite a sight.

He couldn't remember ever having been the lone man in a sea of petticoats and assorted female undergarments.

The camp was just coming to life. Some of the girls were still stumbling from the covered wagons, sleepy-eyed and hungover. A few were sitting near the fires, where a pair of black maids prepared coffee, ham, and eggs for everyone. The scent of the cooking was as pleasing to Fargo's sense of smell as the bevy of females was to his eyes. At this hour, the girls were dressed and behaving functionally, not for work. There were no bangles, no garish, provocative clothing and rouge. Instead, this was a vision of women at their most relaxed and natural. Which meant at their best, to Fargo's way of thinking. He counted eight women in addition to the maids.

The women stared curiously at his arrival. Most of

18

them had a rough-edged appearance that bespoke a life-time spent in the presence of violence. They saw no reason to flee or hide just because a lone man on horseback had intruded on their idyllic scene.

The smell of coffee and breakfast on the cool air of a new day, surrounded by half-naked beautiful women, thought Fargo. *I wonder if this is what heaven is like.*

The young woman who had fired at him was the only one with a weapon. She clutched the rifle and was running toward the women bathing in the river.

"Miss Lacy! Miss Lacy!" The girl was stocky of build, wearing a white petticoat. She was neither pretty nor ugly, but an edge to her country-girl features told of a hard life since leaving the farm. When she became aware of the other girls staring behind her, she whirled and cried out angrily at the sight of him. She started swinging the rifle in his direction. "You dang trespasser, I thought I told you—"

Fargo had already spotted Lacy Jay. She was one of the women bathing nude in the river. He dismounted by swinging his right leg over the Ovaro's head, and landed so abruptly, nose-to-nose with the girl, that she gasped in surprise and stepped back. That's when his right hand whisked the weapon from her.

"And I told you it's too early for target practice," he said evenly, "and I'm no target. Now simmer down, sister. Don't make me throw you in that river to cool you off."

A new voice said, "Relax, Mona. This is a man who'll never do what he's told. Hello, Skye. So you're what the shooting's all about."

Lacy emerged from the river. Stepping ashore, the water running in rivulets down her tawny, shapely body making her nudity glisten radiantly, her form made Fargo entertain the daft notion of a sea goddess rising from the waves. Her chestnut hair was worn down onto her shoulders. She was a little older than the prostitutes in her employ, but Lacy Jay's statuesque beauty was something these younger chickens could only envy, thought

Fargo. Her breasts were full and ripe. Her hips were shaped like an hourglass, and her legs were long and smooth.

He hoped his jaw was not agape.

"Lacy Jay. I reckon it's been a while."

"I reckon." One of her girls stepped forward with a blue silk knee-length wrap, embroidered with an Oriental dragon design. She belted the garment with a nod of thanks. "I hope my doves didn't put a scare into you," she said to Fargo. She turned to Mona. "Honey, this is Skye Fargo."

The young prostitute blinked. "The Trailsman?"

Fargo handed the rifle back to her. "Guilty as charged. Pleased to make your acquaintance, Mona." He turned to Lacy as she approached, her hips moving rhythmically under the clinging silk garment. "She's a good sentry, Lacy Jay. It's not her fault I don't follow instructions. But why post a sentry in the first place? Is it good business to shoot down potential customers?"

Lacy's lively eyes locked with Fargo's. "A lady needs her privacy. That's something you know a whole lot about, isn't it, tall and handsome? How have you been, Skye?"

"Getting by. Heading for the high country. Thought I'd drop by and say howdy."

"Well, howdy back to you, Skye Fargo," said Lacy, and she threw herself into his arms.

It didn't catch him unprepared, and his arms encircled her hourglass figure. He drew her flush against him. The water in the river may have been cool, but there was a wet heat that vibrated from her warm body now. She lifted her mouth for a kiss and when he obliged, the kiss became hot and hungry. Her tongue stabbed into his mouth and her hips churned against him. Up close, her womanly scent caressed his nostrils.

From nearby, some of the whores cheered and whistled.

"That a'way, Lacy Jay!"

Another called out, "Never knew Lacy Jay to help herself to a man!"

There was coarse cackling that reminded Fargo of a henhouse.

When Lacy finally drew back, his body temperature felt as if it had climbed several degrees.

He and Lady hadn't seen each other in years, but their friendship went way back, and so did their peculiar love affair.

Fargo allowed a contented smile to cross his face. "Well now, I reckon stopping by to say howdy wasn't such a bad idea."

Lacy's eyes twinkled. "You can say howdy to me any time, Skye. Say, how's that appetite of yours? You still hungry as a bear first thing in the morning?"

"That I am," he admitted. "Especially after an all-night ride."

She looped an arm through one of his and nodded to the cooking fires.

"Well, settle yourself down and feed the inner man." She leaned close to him and added, for his ears only, "Lord knows I'm going to want some attention from the outside man before you ride out of here, Skye Fargo. Just so you've been warned." Then she realized that several of the nearby women seemed to be leaning forward, attempting to overhear their conversation. "Go on, you bunch of layabouts," Lacy called out in a friendly, big sisterly voice, but commanding just the same. "Today you make a living on your feet, not on your backs. I want to be halfway to Fort Grant by tonight. There's horny soldiers with money at the end of this trail. Those that have eaten, start fixing up the teams. The rest of you get yourselves fed pronto. We break camp in an hour."

There was some mild grumbling, but most of it was good-natured. Activity in the camp took on a more organized rhythm as Fargo and Lacy reached the cooking area.

One of the black women served Fargo a plate heaped high with eggs, ham, and flapjacks.

Fargo found a seat on a log that faced the sunrise. He wolfed down his breakfast, sloshing it down with cup after cup of coffee.

Wisps of clouds over mountains to the east were scarlet with the first rays of the rising sun, becoming pale yellow against a sky turning blue as the sun climbed higher. The air was losing its dawn crispness. It was going to be a hot day.

Lacy sat down next to him and they watched the sunrise in a comfortable, mutual silence for several minutes while he plowed through breakfast.

Fargo was as impressed with her as always. He liked the way Lacy took care of herself. He liked the way she was polite and considerate to those around her, including the black women who she treated as equals. He liked the way she commanded authority over a hard-bitten lot of tough-living women while, at the same time, she was obviously held in high esteem by them.

Lacy waited until he set his cleaned plate aside and was leisurely sipping from his coffee cup.

"I've missed you, Skye." She traced a finger around a lock of his hair that curled over his collar. "Seems like the longer I miss you, the deeper you work yourself into this ol' gal's heart."

"Ol' gal, hell." Fargo admired her openly. "You've got that special something, honey, that everyone of these gals wish they'd been born with. You're still as pretty as a field of sunflowers, and you always will be."

She giggled like a schoolgirl and elbowed him affectionately. "Skye Fargo, you are still one silver-tongued devil."

He leaned over and held her chin, then kissed her. "I'm just improving with age, sweetheart. Just like you."

She gave a throaty laugh. "I like the sound of that." Then her eyes grew serious. "But I'd rather know the truth, Skye. Seems like whenever you ride into my life, it's because you've got your own personal reason for doing it. What's your reason this time?"

His eyes crinkled with humor. "You think you've got your old buddy Skye pretty well figured out, don't you, Lace?"

"Am I wrong?"

He sighed, then decided to dive right in.

"I'm tracking a couple of hardcases named Taggart and Linder." He told her briefly about the job he'd undertaken for G.B. Mandell. "It's a safe bet this girl, Britt, has fallen for one of these rounders, and they're hightailing it back home or to points unknown."

"Once they put enough distance between them and this Mandell gent, they'd split up," said Lacy. "The feller with the gal would head one way. His partner in crime would ride off in the other direction. How am I doing so far?"

"You'd make a good trailswoman," he conceded. "The one who's riding alone, he'd take his cut of the ransom Mandell paid before he lit out. So I started thinking about one rounder on the trail alone, with money. I'm thinking the chances are he'd stop by and spend some of his time and money at Lacy Jay's famous traveling bordello."

"And you'd be right, Skye," said Lacy, "just like you always are." She looked at Mona, sitting on a rock nearby, who'd set her rifle aside and was finishing off a plate of ham and eggs. "Mona, come on over here, hon. This gentleman wants to talk to you about last night."

4

"I didn't like him," said the young whore. "He made me do things that hurt."

Lacy's eyes were compassionate. "You know I don't allow rough stuff in my camp, honey. You could have called out and I would have—"

The girl dropped her eyes.

"He paid me real good, Miss Lucy. I didn't know it was going to hurt so much. Kind of left me in a temper today. Reckon that's why I took it out on this feller," Mona nodded to Fargo, "shooting at him and all, I mean. Guess I just don't much care for men in general this morning."

Fargo grunted. "You'll have to get over that in a hurry, line of work you're in."

Lacy stepped to the girl's side and placed a comforting arm around her.

"Everything's going to be all right," she told the whore. "You ride in the back of one of the wagons until you're feeling better."

"Thank you, Miss Lacy. I'll be feeling better by tonight."

"I know you will, child. And it's a two-day trail to Fort Grant. You just take it easy. But first I want you to answer Mr. Fargo's questions."

"Yes, ma'am." The girl turned to Fargo.

"Did the man tell you his name?" said Fargo.

The girl nodded. "His name is Linder."

"That's him." Fargo stroked his beard thoughtfully. "So it's Taggart who took off with the woman."

"Are you after Mr. Linder?" asked Mona. "He thought he was tough, but, mister, I can tell you're the real thing."

Lacy murmured under her breath, "Amen to that."

"I'm riding him down," said Fargo. "I want to find out where his partner was headed. I figure to make Linder tell me, whether he wants to or not. That's the only lead I've got, unless he said anything to you about a man named Taggart."

"No, sir, he didn't say nothing about nobody. But I want to ask you a favor, mister, if you don't mind."

Fargo grinned. "Why should I mind? Way I look at it, Mona, I owe you a favor. You did me one by firing a warning shot instead of putting a bullet into my brain. What can I do for you?"

She smiled a little smile, the first one Fargo had seen on her face. "You make a gal laugh the way you jape, mister," she said. "But what I'm wanting is serious. When you catch up with this Linder feller, I want you to slug him a good one and tell him it's from that little whore he called dirty names and hurt back at Miss Lacy's. I want him to know that before you lay him out."

"And what makes you think I'm going to lay him out?"

She scrutinized him. "I don't know. You're a nice man, but you look like you could be plumb mean as sin if you set your mind to it, and I've got a feeling that's the way you're going to be when you catch up with that rattlesnake we're talking about. Will you do that for me, Mr. Fargo? Will you hurt him some? And tell him it's for what he did to me."

Fargo made a noncommittal, placating gesture. "Let me find him first. Did he say where he was headed?"

"I can answer that," Lacy interjected. "He was bragging real big when he first rode in, when I was letting him look over the girls before he picked Mona. And he's riding straight into trouble."

25

"He's riding into Indian country," Mona explained to Fargo.

His eyes narrowed. "I heard there was some trouble with hostiles, but I thought it was a good deal east of here."

Lacy nodded. "It is, but that's the way he was riding. He's heading to El Paso. Said he had people there. Tell you the truth, Skye, now that you're here it makes sense."

"What does, Lacy?"

"He was whiskey drunk. Drunk and mean. And he was scared. He kept looking over his shoulder like someone was following him."

"That figures," said Fargo. "Considering the amount of money Mandell's paying me, I'm inclined to believe a rascal like Linder will want to put distance between himself and a powerful man like that. Especially after the way he and Taggart took Mandell for his money, and his bride."

"And his pride," said Lacy. "To a man like your Mr. Mandell, his pride is the most important thing. Men like that can't bear to have it tarnished by someone else."

Mona touched Fargo's sleeve. "You'd better get after him if you don't want him to lose you. He's got a good four-hour start on you, mister."

The Ovaro was contentedly grazing close enough for Fargo to reach over and pat the horse's mane.

"I believe we'll be able to catch up with him."

Lacy took this opportunity to stand. She was statuesque in her lace-fringed blue wrap. The sunlight sparkled off droplets of water in her hair like it was sprinkled with diamonds.

"Come back to my wagon, Skye. I've got some things I want to show you."

Fargo knew an invitation when he heard one. He stood, and tipped his hat to Mona.

"Thank you for your time, miss, and good luck to you."

"You watch your scalp if you're fixing to travel," the prostitute called after him. "We heard tell of ranches and

26

wagon trains being attacked by them hostiles, right, Miss Lacy? Them savages wouldn't think twice about going after one or two men alone out there in the desert. You're the one needs luck, mister, and I hope you got it."

Fargo and Lacy were walking side by side through the camp that had taken on an organized atmosphere as they prepared to travel.

"Cute kid," Fargo commented with a nod back in Mona's direction.

Lacy sniffed. "If you like them green. I thought you preferred grown women."

Hers was the last in the row of covered wagons, well removed from the communal camp area. The backside of the Conestoga was practically flush against the riverbank.

Fargo found his eyes filled with the lovely sight of Lacy Jay's nicely shaped backside as she lifted herself into the wagon. Fargo saw no reason not to climb aboard and follow. He hoisted himself into the wagon's interior.

In the brief instant since she'd disappeared from his sight, Lacy had rolled over onto a bearskin rug that was laid out as a bed beneath colored scarves that adorned the interior of the wagon, turning its drabness into an intimate place perfectly suited for the beautiful woman now stretched out before him.

She rested on her elbows, and had one bare leg extended, the other cocked at the knee. She'd unbelted the front of her wrap. Her chestnut hair spilled down onto her shoulders, some strands draped luxuriously across the milky smoothness of breasts tipped with pink, aroused nipples. The wagon's interior was subtly scented with her musk.

Fargo paused before her, his eyes drinking in the long, lush contours of her perfectly formed figure.

"Do any of those young gals out there," he said, nodding in the direction of the others, "know that I'm the one who named you Lacy Jay?"

She chuckled. "None of them go back that far. Guess that's a sign of how far you and me go back, wouldn't you say?"

Having feasted his eyes on her nudity, savoring her beauty like he might a fine wine, he doffed his hat and unbuckled his gunbelt. He couldn't take his eyes from her. He nodded to the lace at the hem of her wrap. "You like lace, and you're always naked as a jaybird." He tugged off his buckskin shirt.

She leaned forward to help him tug off his boots. Her eyes inventoried his physique.

"Skye, you're still built like the man you always were." A gasp caught in her throat when his britches dropped. Her eyes widened pleasantly at what she saw. Her lips curved into a lascivious smile. "And you're still the best put-together man I've ever set my eyes on."

Having shucked his clothes, Fargo lowered himself to join her on the bearskin rug. She rolled onto her side. He drew her to him, then drew her lips to his. The kiss sizzled, her tongue slithering in and out of his mouth, wet and hot. He brought his free hand up to cup her breasts, squeezing first one, then the other in the way he knew she liked, his thumb ever so lightly brushing across the nipple, stoking her fires.

When the kiss finally broke and they came up for air, Lacy threw her head back, revealing the curve of her throat. She moaned, soft and low, when he began kissing her there. He spoke to her softly between kisses.

"I get the idea from hearing the girls talk that you're not exactly known for being with fellers like this."

She sighed softly and one hand drifted across his chest and lower, exciting him further as her fingers danced across his abdomen and closed around the semihardness of his shaft. She began stroking him with a very loosely held fist.

Fargo found himself holding her steamy nakedness closer, tightening his embrace as she worked him like that.

She brought her lips to his ear. "Why would I want to be with another feller?" she whispered, and her hot tongue darted out to tantalize his ear. "Have you ever considered that I might be more than just fond of you, Skye?"

He honestly hadn't, and he blinked with surprise.

"But, Lacy darlin', we only see each other maybe once a year or so."

Her loosely closed fist continued its up-down jerking motion, making him harder by the second.

"Well." She curved her nakedness even more closely against him. "I'm sure not the first one to observe that love is a strange thing." She glanced down at the full extension of his manhood. She released his member and returned to her laid-back position except that this time, both of her legs were bent at the knee and her legs were spread slightly farther apart than before. "Now do you want what this here girl's offering to you, Mr. Trailsman, or am I going to have to save it for another year until the next time I see you?"

Fargo positioned himself between her legs, saying, "No reason to put off until tomorrow . . ."

She guided his hardness into her and he sunk in to the hilt, eliciting a long, drawn-out groan of pleasure from both of them. His callused hands reached beneath her and cupped the firm orbs of her bottom. His hips thrusting into her, he started pumping hard and fast. She joined her ankles behind his driving hips, and began hammering his back with her fists, her head whipping back and forth, her hair a glistening chestnut spill across the bearskin.

"Oh, Skye! Skye! Yes! Oh my God, I think about you doing this to me every night! Oh, yesss!"

Her fingernails clawed at his back. She bit into his shoulder as a sudden, powerful shudder surged through her. When the spasmodic, uncontrollable bucking of her hips subsided somewhat, he slowed up the pace, but he did not stop. His hips moved from side to side and before long her hips were again jerking hungrily.

"Oh! Oh my goodness! Oh, Skye, you're going to make me come again!"

And he did. And this time, he let himself release and their bodies quaked together in grinding passion.

Some time later, he held her for a while in his arms, stroking her luxuriant chestnut hair while her index finger curled lazily through the hairs on his chest.

29

"I'm surprised you haven't let some rich old rancher make an honest woman out of you, Lacy."

"That wouldn't be very honest of me. I'll settle for you just riding in once a year or so and making a woman out of me. That suit you, Skye?"

He hugged her and kissed the top of her head. "Suits me fine."

5

The terrain was rocky and hilly. The trail skirted the southern tip of the Chiricahua Mountains, wending its way through a scattering of mesquite and juniper trees before crossing a pebble-strewn dry wash. The trail resumed on the opposite side of the wash, at the base of a towering mass of red rock.

Fargo now crouched atop the rock formation.

He tried to ignore the pummeling heat of the high-noon sun that glared down on him. He brushed a sleeve across his forehead, wiping away the sweat. He uncapped his canteen and took a swig of water that was already near the boiling point from having sloshed around inside the metal container throughout the morning's hard ride that had brought him here. He washed the water around in his mouth to clear away the gritty trail dust, then he spat. The water splashed across baking-hot rock, evaporating even before Fargo recapped and set aside the canteen.

He was waiting for Linder from his elevated vantage point. He had seen no movement below except for wildlife. A mountain lion, venturing down to hunt for prey, had ambled past, proud and regal, sniffing along the length of the wash but not sensing his presence. A short time later, a rattlesnake slithered by, very near to him. But the snake had seen no reason to attack or challenge, and continued on away from him.

Luckily, there had been no sign of Indians, hostile or otherwise.

Fargo had a healthy respect for the Apache. They were the true natives of this part of America, as far as he was concerned; the fiercest of warrior tribes. And these mountains, hills, and desert plains were their domain even in the face of military forts intended to provide protection to the white settlements.

Fargo could read sign with the best and could survive in any hostile environment. But this was Apache land, and he never underestimated an adversary. The Apaches' knowledge of this terrain far surpassed his own. And so, while he perceived no Indian presence, he remained vigilantly aware of his surroundings. A surprise attack could come from any direction at any time.

His rifle rested against a rock, close at hand. He'd released the hammer strap of the holster so that the Colt could be drawn fast.

The Ovaro was at the foot of the boulders, waiting patiently on the far side of the boulders, out of sight of the trail.

Fargo heard the *clip-clop* of hooves moments before the rider appeared.

Linder came into view riding a big bay. He drew up at the tree line and looked cautiously in both directions, up and down this stretch of dry wash.

He matched the description provided by Lacy. A swarthy, wiry man, he wore a pistol tied low, gunfighter-style. A cigarillo jutted from a corner of his mouth. He took several puffs on it while he peered in either direction, regarding the open expanse of the wash. He recognized the danger of showing himself, of crossing the wash in the open, and seemed hardly enthusiastic about doing so. But his horse was in a worked-up lather, indicating that Linder was in a hurry to get through Indian country, and was in no mood to turn around now.

After a hesitation of nearly a full minute by Fargo's reckoning, Linder nudged the bay to cross the wash. The metal-on-pebble scrape of the horse's hooves carried to Fargo. Even the horse seemed apprehensive.

Finally, Linder crossed the wash with his hand on the butt of his holstered revolver.

Fargo lowered the length of his body along the red rock. Keeping the horseman in sight, he eased his way across the huge boulder, ready to leap, getting as close as he could get overlooking the trail without risking being seen by Linder.

Fargo sensed a practically audible sigh of relief from man and horse alike when Linder and his bay reached this side of the wash. He lost sight of Linder then, as the trail wound its way uphill, skirting the rock formation. But Fargo's ears gauged the sound of the horse's hooves, and when he estimated that Linder was directly below his position, Fargo made his move.

He leaped at the horseman, springing from the towering boulder as if launched from a catapult.

Linder had only enough time to start to swing around in the direction of the attack from above. The cigarillo dropped from his mouth at the impact of Fargo slamming into him. The velocity of the collision of bodies was forceful enough to tumble both men from the horse. They landed roughly in a cloud of dust.

Fargo jumped to his feet and, following through on the element of surprise, he moved in on Linder. But Linder had a compact, dangerous litheness about him, and even as he came to his feet, he brought his revolver from its holster.

Fargo lifted a boot, delivering a short, sharp kick that sent the pistol careening from Linder's fingers, landing in the dirt well beyond his reach.

Linder backpedaled, then froze with his arms spread wide in a gesture of surrender. "Whoa there, slick." Linder made a poor attempt at sounding cordial. "What the hell is this all about? I think you have the wrong party. We've never met."

"You're going to wish it had stayed that way," said Fargo.

He had not drawn his pistol.

This reassured Linder. He made a minor production of dusting off his jeans and shirt from having been knocked to the ground.

"What the hell is this all about?"

He stepped toward his revolver, extending an arm to retrieve the gun.

Fargo placed his palm on the butt of his Colt.

"Leave it," he said coldly.

The icy tone of command froze Linder in his tracks. He swung back to face Fargo. His eyes narrowed.

"I know what this is about. Mandell sent you. That rich bastard bought himself a tracker to hunt down me and Taggart."

"That's the score." Fargo nodded to the smoking cigarillo that had landed a few inches from the gun. "I hope for our sake that you haven't been smoking much on this trail. An Apache downwind can pick up the scent of tobacco from a quarter-mile away."

"What do you want with me?" Linder demanded. "If Mandell wanted me dead, I'd be dead." He indicated the bay with the stuffed saddlebags. "I've got me a piece of change, mister. Maybe I can buy my way out of this?"

"If all I wanted was your money," said Fargo, "you'd have been dead a few miles back."

Linder eyed Fargo keenly. "Well, what the hell do you want?"

"I want you to tell me where your friend Taggart and his hostage are," snapped Fargo.

"Hostage?" Linder laughed unpleasantly. "Taggart asked me to head north with him and track him down a new wife after his last one killed herself." He chuckled. "Can't say as I blame her. Anyway, he found Britt and, mister, she was in on shaking down that moneybags Mandell right from the start. That girl may be a cool-looking blonde, but Taggart and her was humping each other outside, against the back wall of the restaurant where no one could see, fifteen minutes after they met. They just sort of went plumb loco for each other right off, the way it happens sometimes, you know? I seen them meet. Me and Taggart was going into the hotel restaurant. She was coming out, alone. She just got all attracted to Taggart right off, she did, and Taggart, he went along with it like any man would. He ain't a bad-looking cuss to women,

34

I reckon." Linder chuckled humorlessly. "But I'll tell you this. That stupid little bitch is in over her head."

"Is that right?"

"That's right. I'm glad to get away from Taggart, you want to know the truth. I worked for him, and me and him we rode up to Silver City to look around some. Then this thing happened between them."

"Sounds like this Taggart is real smart."

"Smart enough," said Linder. "And he's mean. He's what you call a sadistic son of a bitch. But that stupid blond foreign bitch, she don't know about that side of him yet." He laughed, a nasty sound. "And it won't be no good for her when she finds out."

"You just reminded of something," said Fargo.

He stepped forward. Before Linder could respond, Fargo delivered a swinging backhand slap with enough punch to knock the man off his feet.

Linder regained his footing, wobbly at first, rubbing one side of his face that was beginning to swell. He wiped away blood that oozed from his mouth. He glared at Fargo.

"What the hell was that for?"

"That was for that little whore you roughed up last night. See, Linder, I think you're a sadistic son of a bitch, just like your buddy."

"The hell with what you think. So you tracked me down. Call the play."

"I already have. You're going to tell me where I can find Taggart and Mr. Mandell's bride-to-be."

"The hell I am," Linder snarled. "You think it's just Mandell I'm lighting out from? I told you, mister, I seen what Taggart's really like. I don't want no part of him no more."

"I don't have time for a lot of palaver. Make it easy on yourself. Tell me what I want to know."

Linder licked his lips. "Are you going to kill me?"

"Not unless I have to."

Linder eyed his fallen pistol. "You know we're in Indian country. I should be armed."

"You should be in the calaboose for stealing money from Mr. Mandell," said Fargo. "But let's not talk about what should be. Let's talk about where I can find Taggart and the woman."

"If I do, will you let me go?"

Fargo shrugged. "Why not? I've got no use for you. I don't even like looking at you."

"All right," said Linder, "but then you've got to let me get the hell out of here. The longer we stay put in one place, the more chance we got of bringing Indians down on us."

Fargo knew that this was true. He perceived no other presence, though he knew this did not necessarily mean that there were no Apaches lurking about.

"Get on with it," he told Linder. "Where's Taggart taking her?"

"A town named Mescal, about a day's ride south of here. The town ain't much, but there's good rangeland all around it. They call it Slaughter Town because there's so much killing."

"There's liable to be more," said Fargo. "Now get on your horse and get out of here."

"You mean that, mister? You're letting me go?"

"I don't ever want to see you in these parts again," Fargo told him. "Do you understand me?"

"You can count on me not coming around," Linder assured him. "It don't pay to have a big man like Mr. Mandell mad at you." He glanced at the saddlebags and chuckled. "That is, it don't pay but once."

"Make tracks," said Fargo.

Linder gulped loudly. "Uh, say, mister, I've got to have my gun, me riding through Indian country."

Fargo's hand remained on the butt on his Colt. "All right."

Linder approached the pistol carefully. When he reached the gun, he half turned, scooped up the pistol, and his demeanor changed as he whirled, swinging the gun up.

"Die, you son of a—" he started to snarl.

Fargo went into a crouch, dodging to the side, unleathering his Colt, and swinging it around. It would be close, but he had the edge.

Linder had barely raised the barrel as Fargo's Colt swung on him. The widening of his eyes said that he knew he was likely to die.

But Fargo never got a chance to fire.

In the taut silence of this life-or-death moment, he heard a low-pitched whistling that sounded somewhat, but not quite, like a bullet speeding past his right ear from behind. There was no gunshot.

A feathered arrow imbedded itself into the center of Linder's chest.

Linder stayed on his feet for a few seconds, stumbling back as if he'd been shoved, his arms flailing out to his sides, his eyes staring in sheer surprise at the arrow protruding from his chest. Blood gushed from his mouth and he went down, dead.

Fargo whirled and threw himself to the ground.

War cries filled the air. Two more arrows had been fired in his direction. One thudded into a tree inches from Fargo, the other came close enough for him to feel the feathers on the shaft graze his arm.

Two Apache braves were visible up the trail. They wore dusty leggings, tunics, and brightly colored tribal feathers. Shouting victoriously, they reached for more arrows.

A rifleshot cracked from another direction, from atop the rock formation where Fargo had been. A bullet geysered up a clump of dirt a few inches to one side of Fargo.

He recognized the sound of the report.

Dammit, he thought angrily. *They're shooting at me with my own rifle!* They'd come up on him and Linder from the far side of the rocks. An Apache was now on top of those rocks, where Fargo had left the Henry, firing down on him while the other two were about to unleash more arrows.

From his prone position, his Colt barked twice in rapid succession.

Both Apaches up the trail spun around as if taking haymakers to the jaw from an invisible fist. They fell back, their bodies disappearing into the brush along the trail.

Another report cracked from the Henry. And another clump of earth geysered, this time to Fargo's opposite side.

He twisted onto his back and fired up in the direction of the rifleman, but he was firing blindly into the sun, unable to see what he was shooting at. The war whoop from told him that he'd missed. But the rifle fire ceased as the Apache jumped back to avoid Fargo's bullet.

Fargo took this opportunity to roll his way toward the rock formation. He came flush against its base in the shadows, blocked from view of the shooter above him. He started moving quickly around the rocks, toward the rear where he had left the Ovaro.

Within a few paces, another Apache came at him, this one without a war cry to betray his approach. A wide-bladed knife was held high. Fargo fired from the hip. The heavy round from the Colt knocked the Apache into a backward death sprawl, and Fargo continued on.

The first thing he looked for was the Ovaro, and he sighed with relief when he saw the stallion, unharmed. The Ovaro's head was up, sniffing the air, aware that everything was wrong, confused, waiting for a command from Fargo.

Fargo paused at the base of the rocks and reloaded the Colt. He could hear war cries back and forth, which meant that there was the Apache with Fargo's rifle and at least one other. The remaining Apaches were obviously trying to formulate some sort of strategy.

Fargo picked up a handful of pebbles from around his boots. While the Apaches were shouting to each other, certain that they had him cornered, he flung the pebbles.

It was an old trick but, considering the way he was thinning their ranks, the Apache with his rifle would rather be safe but sorry.

The Henry hammered from the rock ledge overhead, and Fargo heard the bullet rustle the underbrush where he'd tossed the pebbles.

That was his cue.

He launched himself from his cover, back into the clearing, in the brief time it was taking the rifleman to chamber another round.

The Apache looked down, saw the sudden apparition that had appeared below, and started to leap back from the line of fire, but not fast enough.

Fargo fired two rounds and they both hit the Apache in the chest. He spun around in a pirouette and sprawled onto the red rock, the Henry flying from his hands, dropping through space. Fargo took a step forward, lifted his left arm, and caught the rifle in one hand.

He heard war cries and galloping hooves from behind him. He spun, keeping low, making as small a target of himself as possible. He holstered the Colt and brought the Henry into firing position, completing the job of chambering another round.

Two Apaches were riding their ponies at him, hellbent for leather, from separate directions. They were whooping it up and each held a lance decorated with tribal war feathers. Sharpened steel points glinted murderously in the sunshine.

The Henry roared.

The Apache to his left was knocked from the saddle, as if jerked by an invisible rope. He hit the ground and did not move. His pony wandered aimlessly.

The other horseman stormed directly at him, the oncoming lance aimed at Fargo. He fired, but the Apache saw it coming and leaned sideways atop his mount without slowing. What should have been a head shot missed him completely.

Then the horseman was upon him.

Fargo leaned sideways and blocked the lance with his rifle. He succeeded in deflecting the blow as the Apache rode past but, in the process, the lance wrenched the rifle from his grip.

As the rifle dropped from Skye's grasp, the Apache pulled up his pony and came at Fargo for another run. He expected Fargo to dodge and compensated with the angle of the lance as he thundered on.

Fargo stood his ground. There was no time for him to

retrieve his rifle or unholster the Colt. The lunging thrust of the lance by the passing horseman missed him by inches. He bent sideways at the waist, gripping the thrust lance with both hands. With his boots dug in solidly, he jerked back hard.

The Apache was yanked from his pony and slammed to the ground. The impact of his fall jarred loose his grip on the lance.

Fargo executed a sharp twisting motion and wrestled the lance from the brave's hands. He whipped it around even as the Apache was unsheathing a knife, leaping at Fargo.

Fargo grunted a primal snarl and lunged, and the tip of the spear pierced the brave's heart.

The Apache grasped the lance now protruding from his chest with both hands. He stumbled back a few steps, just as Linder had.

Fargo released his hold on the lance.

The Apache coughed blood. He fell to the ground, and did not move. The feathered lance pointed skyward from his body like a flagpole.

The abrupt silence was deafening.

Fargo hurried over to retrieve his rifle. The Ovaro cantered over to him, and he mounted up. Fargo scanned his surroundings with his eyes and with the muzzle of his rifle. He detected no other human presence in the area.

It was time to move on.

He rode over to where Linder's bay grazed in tall grass under a mesquite tree. The two horses got acquainted while he relieved Linder's horse of its twin saddlebags. He opened them and peered inside. He whistled softly when he saw the tightly packed wads of money. He refastened the clasps and fastened the saddlebags to his own gear.

Then he rode away.

6

The stage station was a small, empty compound, formed by an adobe main building, corrals, and a ramshackle stable, set on a lonesome stretch of trail in a wide valley not far from the Mexican border. Except for a few scrawny mesquites, there was not a tree in sight. But at dusk, with its lighted windows a burnished gold against the encroaching darkness of night and a plume of smoke curling from an outdoor brick stove, it looked downright inviting to Fargo after a hard day's ride.

He'd started the day with Lacy Jay, had tracked down Linder, and fought for his life at the red rocks, then rode south nonstop, intending to camp out, when he'd come upon this stage station out here in the middle of nowhere.

As Fargo rode slowly into the yard, he called out, "Hello the house!"

A man appeared in the doorway, holding a double-barreled shotgun. The barrels were aimed at Fargo.

"Good evening," Fargo said congenially, as if a gun were not aimed at him.

"Who are you?" the man demanded. "What do you want?"

He was shabbily dressed, in his thirties, with an un-trimmed salt-and-pepper beard. In striking contrast to his appearance, he spoke with the measured cadence of an aristocrat.

Fargo tried delivered his best disarming smile. "I'm

just a pilgrim on the road of life. It's really not necessary to point that gun at me, mister."

"We'll see if it is or not. I asked you what you want."

"Reckon I was hoping you'd let me put up my horse for a night. It's been a long day for him and me and he's served me well. He deserves to be treated right." Fargo patted the horse's mane with gruff affection. "Course, I was hoping you'd allow me to bed down, too."

The man still had not lower the shotgun.

"I send people on their way if I don't like the look of them. This property belongs to the Overland Stage Company. It's my responsibility to keep out riffraff."

"I'm not riffraff, sir. My name is Skye Fargo."

A hesitation, then the station man lowered the shotgun.

"Do tell." He considered Fargo's bearded face and the lithe, six-foot, muscular frame encased in buckskin. "You fit his description, right enough. I've heard of you, sir. You have the reputation of an honest man, and a dangerous one."

"I'd be much obliged if you'd let me and my horse rest up for the night," said Fargo. "I can pay."

"Don't want your money. If what I've heard about you is true, sir, you've been responsible for a fair share of good deeds in the course of your travels."

"The only thing I'll brag about," said Fargo with a smile, "is my modesty."

The man stepped from the porch. "In any event, it is my pleasure to extend our hospitality to you, sir. My name is Brand. Lucius Brand."

Fargo dismounted.

They shook hands. The man's handshake was firm.

"Pleased to meet you, Mr. Brand."

A young woman of about nineteen came walking briskly around the corner of the house from the direction of the outdoor stove. She was drying her hands on her apron.

A little mutt of a dog was yapping merrily at her heels.

"Oh dear, Father," she was saying as she came into view, "I'm afraid I've burned the—" Her voice faltered. She drew up short when she saw Fargo. "Oh, I'm sorry."

"Mr. Fargo," said Brand, "this is my daughter. Emmy, I want you to meet Mr. Fargo. He'll be staying with us for tonight."

She was blond, wide-eyed, rosy-cheeked, with a shapely figure and a childlike freshness about her that was the nubile embodiment of blossoming womanhood.

"Pleased to meet you, Mr. Fargo."

Fargo was smart enough not to be overly cordial to the young lady, what with her father standing at his side scrutinizing him and awaiting his response.

"Pleased to meet you, miss."

Her eyes widened when she got a look at his horse. "Oh my, what a gorgeous animal! An Ovaro, isn't he?"

"Yes, he is," said Fargo. "He's looked better. He's had a long, rough day."

She stepped to the horse and touched it in a way that made the Ovaro snort contentedly.

"I'll brush and groom him if you'll let me."

Fargo chuckled at the way the Ovaro was responding to her attentions like an affectionate colt.

"Appears to me that horse of mine wouldn't have it any other way," he grinned. "If it's okay with your father, that is."

"It's all right with me," said Brand. "Go ahead, daughter."

The girl beamed. "Thank you, Father." Then she frowned. "I, uh, I'm afraid that I've I burnt dinner again. I'm sorry, but one of these days I *will* be as good a cook as Mother was, I promise."

Brand sighed mightily. "That's all right, child. I know you will. It will be beef jerky again tonight. Does that sound like a suitable repast to you, sir?" he asked Fargo with a small smile.

Fargo returned the smile with a nod. "It's the company that matters to me, and I think I got lucky tonight on that score."

He and Brand watched the girl lead the Ovaro off to the stable, the little dog yipping happily after them.

Brand cleared his throat. "A word, if I might, Mr. Fargo, strictly man to man and I mean no offense—"

"None taken," said Fargo. "And don't worry, Mr. Brand. You're offering me a place to rest and a place to sleep. I'll not repay your hospitality by paying undue attention to your daughter."

"Thank you, sir. I should have known you were a gentleman in such matters. My little Emmy, she's at that age. I've been doing the best I could since her mother died. We came out here because of Abigail's health, but . . . that wasn't enough."

"I'm sorry," said Fargo.

"I thought about taking Emmy back home to Virginia. That's what my family wants. But Abigail is buried here, Mr. Fargo. That makes a difference, doesn't it?"

Fargo tried not to show that he was somewhat taken aback by this sudden show of forwardness. He judged Brand to be well bred, intelligent, and achingly lonely at this remote outpost.

"A person's got to go where their heart tells them," Fargo replied. "Course, it doesn't hurt to keep an eye over your shoulder in case someone's trying to get the drop on you."

"What keeps me sane," said Brand conversationally, "is the stream of passengers aboard the stages that stop here, one heading east, the other west. Funny thing, the folks heading west, they've always got themselves a whole lot to say. But the ones heading back to civilization, leaving all this behind after doing their time, they're the ones worth listening to." He again cleared his throat. "I hope you'll not think me out of line, Mr. Fargo."

"How's that, Mr. Brand?"

"May I be permitted a personal question?"

It was generally considered a breech of Western etiquette to inquire of a person's background.

"I owe you for putting me up," said Fargo, "and for your girl taking care of my horse. What do you want to know?"

"Mister, you look tough clear through. Mean enough to bite a snake in two. I guess I'm wondering why you're in these parts. I know most everybody, from talking to the drivers. What's Skye Fargo doing down near the border?" Brand averted his eyes from Fargo's. He brought out a pipe and a pack of tobacco. "Uh, you feel free to tell me to go to blazes and mind my own business if you've a mind to."

"That's all right," said Fargo. "Reckon I look mean because I'm wore out. I had to kill some fellers today. But as a matter of fact, Mr. Brand, I was fixing to try and find a way to get around to just that subject with you. I was hoping to ask you a few questions. A stage stop is always the best place for information, after a hot springs or a whorehouse."

Brand chuckled. He tapped tobacco into his pipe bowl. He struck a match, drawing on the pipe. He shook the match and dropped it, and exhaled a plume of pleasant aromatic smoke. "Well, now that we understand each other, what sort of questions were you going to ask me?"

"I'm here on business," said Fargo. "I'm hunting someone."

"I heard you did that."

"I've looking for a man and a woman."

Brand nodded. "I'm guessing that they passed through here today," said Brand. "You're about five hours behind them, if I'm thinking of the right couple."

"Were they riding a stage?"

"No, sir. They were on horseback. That's why it struck me as strange. And because of who he was. They spent an hour here. Emmy saw to their horses. I fed them." Brand gave Fargo a sideways look. "As you may have guessed, Emmy is not much of a cook though she tries to be, bless her heart. But while I was serving up the stew, Mr. and Mrs. Taggart did not talk much, to each other or to me."

Fargo frowned. "Mrs. Taggart?"

"I assumed her to be so, from the familiarity between them." Brand nodded, took another puff, self-contented. "You recognize the name. I was right. They're the ones you're after."

"You said they didn't talk much."

"They did not. They were, uh, amorously involved with each other. I suppose indiscreet would be the proper term. Suffice to say, I forbade my daughter from witnessing the way Taggart and the woman carried on at the table. They kissed. He fondled her, sir, and she permitted it with good humor. A revolting public display." Brand tapped out the pipe's blackened contents on the heel of his left boot.

"Mrs. Taggart's real husband-to-be wants her brought home," said Fargo.

"I see." Grand pocketed the pipe. "Clear as mud," he added wryly.

"The woman—is she blond, foreign, and beautiful?"

"That would be the woman I speak of," said Brand. You will catch up with them tomorrow."

"What about Taggart?" said Fargo. "Did you know him before he came here today?"

"No, but I knew of him." Brand's leathery face creased. "Taggart is one of the two wealthiest cattle men in the territory. He's like a feudal baron, and his spread is not more than one day's ride south of here."

"That would be around the town of Mescal?"

Brand nodded yes. "Mr. Taggart and Mr. Yates, they're the biggest ranchers in these parts. Fact is, around Mescal, they're the only ranchers. All the little spreads were driven out or just plain went under. There are some ranchers that run herds that Mr. Taggart or Mr. Yates owns. Like I said, feudal barons, the both of them."

"And how do these two powerful men get along with each other?"

"Like dog and cat. I've never met Mr. Yates. But when Mr. Taggart was here, he was in a light frame of mind, but I did not miss the sharp edge just below the surface, if you get my meaning. Mr. Taggart is a mankiller. I saw it in his eyes and I heard it in his voice even when he spoke of foolish things with the woman. Taggart and Yates would each like to be the only land baron in this territory. They are vicious and it is said that they hate each other, and would see each other dead if they could."

"I haven't been through here before or I would have heard of them," said Fargo. "Taggart strayed off his range."

"I heard that he and that no-account, Linder, went on a hunting trip up north."

Fargo nodded. "What they caught was the woman you refer to as Mrs. Taggart."

"Do tell."

"Is there a lawman in Mescal?"

Brand made a rude sound. "If you want to call old Tap Wiley that, if only because he wears a sheriff's badge. But he's about as much a lawman as my daughter's little dog."

"Which one owns the sheriff?"

"That would be Mr. Taggart."

"Then he's the most powerful of the two."

"Granted," said Brand, "but if you're heading that way, you'll find Yates a force to be reckoned with as well. They are the reason the railroad went through. The town went up because the trains needed a place to tank up with water."

Fargo nodded, understanding further why he hadn't heard of Mescal. Some places in the West were growing so fast, boomtowns sprang up practically overnight.

"I'm heading that way in the morning," he said. "But for right now, I'd like to pay you for that information you just gave me."

Brand waved a hand. "No need for that."

"It's not just that," grinned Fargo. "I'm hungry. It's mighty nice of your daughter to tend to my horse the way she is. If you would be kind enough to show me to your outdoor stove and the fixings, and I'll rustle up some eats for all three of us. I haven't met a seasoned old single gent like me yet who couldn't outcook a spring chicken like that little girl of yours."

Taggart and Britt rode into the miner's campsite at dusk.

Britt was exhausted. She and Taggart had covered many miles under the burning sun. She rode a spirited gray mare, a handsome horse that had belonged to G.B. Mandell. She had "liberated" the horse before leaving Silver City with her "kidnapper," Cal Taggart.

The sky to the west was deep purple and the stars were winking overhead. Mountains to the east were limned in silver, preceding a moonrise.

The miner rose from tending his campfire and turned to greet them. He was in his late twenties, Britt judged. There was a good-natured robust quality about him even though his clothes were caked with desert dust, as were the lenses of his thick spectacles. He squinted at the approaching riders, reaching for a rifle that leaned against a boulder, though he kept its muzzle aimed at the ground. Britt saw a packmule tied to a tall ocotillo bush. The animal's load—shovel, pickax, supply packs—was neatly stacked nearby.

"Howdy, mister," said Taggart, with a friendly wave.

Cal Taggart was forty years old, a sandy-haired, handsome six-footer who tipped the scales at two hundred pounds, every inch of it muscle.

Britt knew this from intimate experience. The dangerous-looking, hard-bitten, powerful man had sexually fired her up at the instant of their first encounter.

Since her birth overseas until her arrival in Silver City, America to become the mail-order bride of a wealthy, unattractive, boring businessman, Britt had observed her own life as an existence scripted by others, as if she were an actress taking direction from those around her.

The restlessness to break free of this prison had been building within her for a year, but she had not known what to do about it until dangerous, wild Cal Taggart had entered her life in that hotel restaurant in Silver City less than a week ago.

And of course he had entered *her* less than an hour after their meeting! She felt a blush touch her cheeks at the memory, but told herself that she would have changed nothing. Cal had allowed her to feel like a bird freed from a cage even though the danger in him was never far beneath the surface.

He'd suggested the phony kidnap scheme to her after she became addicted to the way he made her feel with his strong body and knowing ways. He had the stamina of a stallion, and the slyness of a fox.

Their time together since leaving Silver City had continued to pass pleasantly, especially after they parted ways with Linder, whom she found unpleasant. Britt enjoyed riding, and always had. Taggart chose trails leading south, giving a wide berth to the country where hostile Apache roamed.

But in the time since their stop at the stage station, she'd seen a change come over the man she thought she'd fallen in love with. Conspiring to swindle G.B. Mandell had seemed to her at first to be a crazy lark, undertaken by two impulsive people madly in love with each other. That's what she felt for Cal, as recently as their lunch at the stage station, where Taggart had continued to be his handsome, boyishly charming self, a dark physical passion crackling constantly between them.

But since then, she'd noticed a cold remoteness begin to claim him, a change that was subtle at first, but she now sensed it in the phoniness of his amiable greeting to the miner.

Her eyes shifted beside her. Taggart's jaw was set in a way she hadn't seen before, and his smile didn't reach his eyes, reminding her of cold chips of black marble.

Apprehension slithered through her, tightening around her stomach and throat.

When the miner saw that one of the riders was a woman, he set his rifle aside and stepped forward with a friendly smile.

"Howdy, folks. You're the first people I've seen in three weeks of prospecting."

Britt found her voice, telling herself that the strange sensation was born of fatigue.

"Hello. Pleased to meet you, sir. My name is Britt, and this is my husband Cal."

"Pleased to meet you, I'm sure," the young man beamed. "My name is Jacob Jacoby. Please, don't make fun of it. I always tell people that my parents weren't very imaginative."

Taggart dismounted. "Much obliged."

Britt smiled. "Pleased to meet you, Mr. Jacoby."

She liked the young man right off, and she was struck

again at what a wide variety of people she had encountered since coming out West. The only common thread was that everyone was from somewhere else.

"The pleasure's all mine," Jacoby beamed. "I've got some vittles left if you care to join me. I need to brush up on my conversational skills. I have a wife and two small children waiting for me in Mescal."

Taggart said, "You must have gotten lucky out in those hills."

The miner's eyes narrowed, becoming wary. "Why would you say that, mister?"

Taggart nodded to the packs set next to the mule.

"You're heading home because you found yourself some. You don't look to me like a man who would give up until he got what he was looking for."

The miner shifted his weight. His fingers inched closer to his nearby rifle.

"I wouldn't know what you're talking about, mister."

"It don't matter what you know," said Taggart his icy grin spreading. "Because you're dead."

He drew the revolver from its holster at his hip, and triggered a single round. The gunshot cracked dully in the wide-open space.

The bullet struck the miner in the center of the chest. Jacoby was lifted off his feet, into a wide-armed fall. He landed with a thud.

Britt screamed, *Oh my God!*

She leaped from her horse and flung herself to the side of the fallen man.

Jacoby was shuddering, as if from cold. He stared up at her. His eyes were glazing, and a pool of blood was spreading beneath him. He tried to lift an arm and say something. He coughed blood, then his head fell sideways, and he died.

Britt leaped to her feet. She whirled to face Taggart.

He stood with his back to her, having retrieved something from the supply packs stacked beside the mule. He held up the sack that fit snugly in the palm of his hand.

"There it is. Silver. The boy did find himself some."

She stood there for a moment, stunned into immobility by shock and horror.

"But why did you kill him?" she wailed. "You told me that you are a man of money, a successful rancher. Why did you need whatever pittance this poor man has scraped from the earth?"

Taggart hefted the pouch and grunted his satisfaction. He slipped the pouch into his shirt.

"You can never have too much silver, darlin'. I'd think a big girl like you would know that no matter where she's from."

"But . . . but, Cal! This man had a wife and children!"

Taggart snarled and backhanded her across the mouth, jarring her from her feet.

"I reckon it's time you learned the value of a dollar, little lady. How the hell do you think I got to be the most powerful man in the territory?"

The world around her was spinning and blurred. She was more stunned than injured. She lay there upon the hard ground, at his feet. She instinctively brushed away a strand of blond hair. She touched the back of her hand to her lip, and the hand came away with a droplet of her blood.

"You're an animal!" she snarled back at him, rage overcoming her fear and pain. "You're nothing but murdering scum!"

"No, you're wrong," said Taggart in an unusually quiet voice. "I happen to be lord and master of this here land. And right now, you smart-mouthed foreign bitch, you are going to learn another lesson. This one is about respect." Taggart started undoing the leather belt around his waist until it dangled from his hand like a slavemaster's whip. "And I implore you, don't make me have to teach you this lesson a second time, girl. I might kill you by mistake."

He began flogging her with the belt.

7

About noon the following day, Fargo rode into the camp-site and found the miner's body.

He used the dead man's pickax and shovel to dig a shallow grave. It was not easy digging, and Fargo was bare-chested and sweating by the time he finally laid the man to rest. He used the man's tent as a shroud. After the earth had been patted back into place, he covered the gravesite with rocks as a precaution against coyotes or javelinas digging up the body.

When he was done, Fargo stood there, his hat in his hands, staring down at the fresh grave.

"Rest in peace, Jacob. Go with your God. I'll see that your missus gets your personal effects."

He could think of nothing else to say. He had searched the man's belongings for identification, and had found a personal journal, including a daguerreotype of an attractive woman and two young children, and clear reference to their residence in Mescal. These now resided in Fargo's saddlebag. He turned from the grave. His work here was done. He took a sip from his canteen, looped by its strap from the Ovaro's saddle horn.

The stallion was enduring the company of the mule that remained tethered to the ocotillo.

Fargo had instructed his horse to stay, and the Pinto had obeyed, for which he was now rewarded with a hand-ful of grain. Fargo spilled some grain for the mule to munch on.

His first priority, upon arriving on the scene, had been to bury Jacob. Buzzards and other scavengers had already been at the body, and a man's dignity should be preserved in death, to Fargo's way of thinking. But he had not wanted the Ovaro wandering around. He wanted this ground to remain as it had been when last trod upon.

He recapped the canteen, then stooped low and started studying the ground, reading sign. He knelt to one knee from time to time to scrutinize. After some ten minutes of this, he had a fair idea of what had transpired here.

No Apaches had been involved, for one thing. He'd known that at first sight of the body. The Apache disfigured the bodies of their enemy, and Jacoby's only harm by human hand—which had been more than enough—was a bullet through the chest. Additionally, the hoofprints of only two horses were apparent, and these were shod. The Apache traveled in war parties, and their ponies were unshod.

Of course, this could have been the work of Apaches who simply hadn't felt the inclination to hack up Jacoby, and who had been riding stolen U.S. mounts. But Fargo didn't think so, considering the condition of the ground not far from the body, where some sort of frantic activity had taken place. He studied what footsteps he could discern, identifying the separate imprints of a man and a woman, both wearing boots. He was able to distinguish the difference by noting discrepancies like depth of an imprint, indicating weights and body mass, as did a comparison of the length of step.

He returned to the Ovaro for another swig from the canteen, sloshing the water around inside his parched mouth and spitting it out.

This was the work of Taggart. Fargo was closing in on the man and the "kidnapped" mail-order bride. But going by the sign Fargo had near the spot where he'd found Jacoby, he now believed that Britt had not been party to the murder of Jacob Jacoby. There were signs of a struggle, as if someone had thrashed terribly upon the ground. For Fargo, there was only one way to read it. Britt had found herself in over her head, but too late to save the hapless miner. And when she and Taggart left here, she was his prisoner, not his partner.

Fargo swung astride the Ovaro, leaning over to fetch the mule's reins. Taking the animal along would slow him, but he could surely sell a healthy beast of burden to among the first of the passersby he would encounter on the trail to Mescal, and he would give the money from the sale to Jacoby's widow. And Fargo reminded himself that, based on Lucius Brand's estimation of the distance, he was already a couple of hours or less from the Taggart ranch.

The preceding night, spent with the Brands at the stage station, had been pleasant. Emmy did a professional job of grooming and caring for the Ovaro and bubbled enthusiastically over dinner about her love of horses and her interest in pursuing a career as a veterinarian. For his part, Mr. Brand had mostly contented himself with rocking in his rocker on the porch, puffing his pipe, and appeared to simply revel in the comfortable flow of conversation. He and Emmy both appreciated the fact that Fargo behaved more like an older brother to Emmy, rather than as an older man with a lecherous eye for a blossoming young gal. This morning, Fargo had taught Emmy the secrets of making flapjacks. From the way the Ovaro acted visibly hesitant about leaving, Fargo couldn't help but note aloud that Emmy obviously had a friend for life in the big steed.

He then rode off from the stage station at a gallop, just past sunrise, with a backward wave to Mr. Brand and his daughter who stood in the shadow of the ramshackle adobe structure and returned his farewell wave.

It was another blistering hot day.

Now, hours after leaving the Brands, he kneed the Ovaro into a trot away from the miner's final resting place, leading the surprisingly obedient mule.

There was no great hurry now. Fargo's job was to bring home a mail-order bride to Mr. G.B. Mandell. He had established where she was. If she had refused to go with Taggart from here, her body would have been stretched out in the sun alongside Jacob Jacoby's. Instead, after considerable resistance, she had accompanied Taggart. A man like Taggart wouldn't let such a hard-won prize out of his sight for long. So Fargo knew where the woman was. And he knew what his job was.

Taggart had murdered Jacob Jacoby in cold blood, leaving behind a widow and small children, judging from what Fargo had gleaned from Jacoby's journal.

Thinking about this and the treatment endured by a defenseless woman at the scene of Jacoby's murder made Fargo's mouth draw into an angry line, made his knuckles whiten around the reins.

He didn't like men such as Cal Taggart, who did things like that. To Fargo's way of thinking, the world would be a far better place without them.

That afternoon, Fargo reined in the Ovaro at the foot of the steps leading to the porch surrounding the Taggart ranch house.

As expected, he'd freed himself of the mule, selling it to a prospector who told Fargo that the trail to Mescal cut across the Taggart range.

Fargo had continued on, eventually encountering some cowboys tending a herd. They'd been friendly enough since he offered them each some of his good tobacco to roll their own smokes. Good tobacco was not always easy to come by out here, and Fargo packed it as much for himself as to occasionally loosen tongues. The cowboys confirmed that he as on the Bar-40 spread, owned by Cal Taggart. He'd thanked them and rode on, passing more and more herds and rich grazing land rimmed by mesas.

A common denominator he noted about Taggart's hired hands that he saw was that every man wore a revolver, the holster strapped low to the hip. The average cowboy might carry a holstered revolver, but in most cases a rifle was preferable in situations where self-defense with deadly force was required, whether the predator was man or beast. But the fact that Taggart's men all looked like seasoned gunfighters impressed Fargo at what a formidable force he was up against in extricating the woman named Britt and returning her to his client. A conservative estimate, formulated by the time he'd drawn up to the porch at the ranch house, put the odds against him at about fifty to one.

With all of the comings and goings about the busy ranch, especially here at its center in the yard formed by the house, barns, corrals, and assorted sheds, no one had bothered to stop or question him.

There was a bustle of late-afternoon activity about the yard. A Chinese cook and his staff were prepping for dinner at the outdoor oven adjacent to the main house. Cowboys were unsaddling their horses, and Mexican ranch hands were leading the horses to the stables, while a wagon team bearing supplies trekked in, trail dust caking man, beast, and wagons like sooty gray flour.

Reining the Ovaro to a halt, Fargo was about to hail the house when a screen door slammed outward.

A woman stormed onto the porch. She flew down the steps and ran in Fargo's direction.

This could only be Britt, he told himself.

Sky-blue eyes complemented her Nordic cheekbones and over-ripe lips. Blond tresses fell onto her shoulders, shimmering as she ran.

When she reached him, he looked down her, from atop the horse, and said, "Afternoon, ma'am. I was wondering if—"

She clung to him, staring up at him with beseeching eyes.

"You must help me," she rasped with a heavy accent. "Please! Whoever you are, you must help me!"

From inside the house, a voice thundered. "Dammit, Duff! That bitch got away. Get her back in here!"

"I'll get her, Mr. Taggart," a voice replied. "She seen somebody ride up!"

The screen door slammed again.

The man who stepped out this time wore the clothing of a working cowboy and, like the others Fargo had seen, a pistol rode low on his hip for a quick draw. Duff was in his twenties. His hair was shaggy and his thin lips were twisted into a permanent sneer. He left the porch in a bound and crossed toward Britt.

She was tugging at Fargo's buckskin leggings. "They're holding me prisoner! Don't leave without helping me, I beg of you."

Duff jerked her sharply. She almost lost her balance, but his hold kept her upright.

"What the hell do you think you're doing?" he snarled. "You'll be lucky if Mr. Taggart don't bury you up to your neck in sand with red ants, the way the Apaches do. It takes a person days to die like that."

She struggled. "Let go of me!"

He tightened his hold and sneered. "I wouldn't mind seeing you die like that," he hissed, spraying her with his saliva. "I ain't liked women but for one thing ever since mama kicked me out when I was ten."

"Appears to me your mama waited ten years too long," Fargo said quietly from astride the Ovaro.

Duff froze in his tirade. He didn't release the woman, but he glared at Fargo.

"And who might you be, trail bum? And what the hell makes this any of your business?"

A third man had appeared. He stepped from the house and positioned himself on a porch step, surveying this tableau.

Cal Taggart's polished boots, pressed slacks and shirt, and black string tie, worn with a long corduroy jacket, made him look every inch the gentleman land baron. He was smoking a cheroot.

"You might also ask the gentleman," he told Duff in a bemused tone, "what the hell is he's doing on Cal Taggart's spread in the first place."

The blonde had stopped struggling, obviously realizing the futility of an escape attempt. She studied Fargo with great interest.

Duff had not released his hold of her wrist. "You heard Mr. Taggart," he sneered at Fargo. "Explain yourself, trail bum."

Fargo studied the man for protracted seconds, as if

clinically studying a bug. Then he turned to Taggart and asked dispassionately, "Who the hell is this clown?"

Duff sputtered. "Clown?" Outrage visibly shook him. He released Britt, shoving her away, whirling to face Fargo, his arm bent, his hand hovering at his gun, ready to draw.

"You smart-mouthed—"

Fargo tensed, ready for anything. Ready to draw. Ready to leap. Ready to throw a knife. Anything could happen in the next instant.

"Duff, stop it." Taggart's command snapped like the crack of a whip. "Stand down, damn you. I'll have no gunplay in my yard."

Duff stood with knees bent, fingers quivering as if they itched to draw the revolver from its holster. "But, Mr. Taggart—"

Taggart left the porch. "Stand down, I said."

Duff glared a killing hatred at Fargo but relaxed his posture, his fingers no longer hovering so near the butt of his pistol.

Taggart took a final draw on the cheroot and flicked it aside. "I would choose my words more carefully when addressing Mr. Duff."

Fargo nodded at Duff. "I wasn't addressing him at all. I was addressing you."

Duff's features reddened. But he said and did nothing.

Taggart chuckled. "You do not seem to be in the habit of backing down, mister."

"Only when I'm wrong." Fargo looked at Duff. "Sorry we had to have words." He indicated Britt, who was massaging the arm where she'd been held. "I just don't like seeing the fairer sex mishandled."

Duff's eyes blazed. "I don't want no apology from you, you piece of cow dung. I'd take you apart if Mr. Taggart told me to."

"It appears," Taggart said pointedly to Fargo, "that we all know each other's name except yours, mister."

Fargo dismounted to stand, facing them. He decided to tell half of the truth. "People call me Skye," he told Taggart.

Taggart threw a thumb in Britt's direction. "Well, Skye, I'll let you in on a little secret. That woman belongs to me just like that ground you're standing on and the air you're breathing."

Fargo inhaled the crispness of approaching night.

"You're not going to charge me for this fine night air, are you, Mr. Taggart?" There was a trace of insolence in his voice.

Duff spat. "You ain't going to be breathing it for much longer, no account. I'm looking forward to killing you, hombre. You got a right smart mouth."

Fargo became aware that the activity had ceased around them in the yard. A dozen or more sets of eyes watched. A half-dozen hands were close to holstered pistols.

Taggart withdrew a fresh cheroot from his breast pocket.

"It seems the time has come when I decide whether you live or die, Mr. Skye. Say, that's got kind of a ring to it, don't you think?" He struck a match on his thumb and watched Fargo through the smoke as he got the cigar going. "What'll it be, cowboy? Duff was only doing what I told him to do, fetching my woman here back inside the house, weren't you, Duff?"

"Yes, sir, Mr. Taggart."

"There, you see. It doesn't matter what the woman wants," said Taggart. "The only thing matters is what I want, because I'm God Almighty around here." He eyed Fargo closely through the smoky haze curling from his cheroot. "You have a problem with that, Skye?"

Fargo averted his face from the pathetic, pleading eyes of the woman.

He could not possibly fight and rescue her right now, not given these odds. And so he went with a notion that he'd been planning since riding up to the ranch house.

"Way I see it, Mr. Taggart, every man's private business is his own private business."

Taggart smirked. "Mighty sensible answer. I like your style, mister. You've got a cool hand, but you look like you can burn hot enough."

"I'm looking for a job," said Fargo. "That's why I'm here. I heard you were looking for hands who knew how to punch cows and use a gun."

"You know how to handle a gun, eh?" Taggart lifted an eyebrow.

"I do."

"Well, I believe that. And your fists? Can you handle those?"

"I can."

"Let's find out," said Taggart. "Duff. Take him."

With the roar of a charging bull, Duff came at Fargo so fast, Fargo didn't have time to dodge.

8

Duff slammed into Fargo with his head lowered, the top of that head ramming into Fargo's stomach, driving the breath from him as he was knocked to the ground. Duff tumbled down on top of him, the man's big hands reaching for Fargo's throat, grabbing like claws.

Fargo landed, keeping his body limber so that, with the murderous cowboy atop him, he could bring his knees together and upward into Duff's chest. Duff exhaled sharply and was flipped over and away from Fargo.

Both men came to their feet simultaneously and went at each other with fists up and swinging. Some cheers and taunts came from those witnessing the fight.

Fargo planted himself firmly and blocked a right with a raised left. Then he popped Duff one, two, three times to the jaw in rapid succession while holding onto the front of Duff's shirt with his left hand. Duff remained standing, taking the punches, his eyes rolled back in his head. Fargo released the shirtfront, and Duff collapsed into an inert lump at his feet.

Fargo looked around and caught sight of Britt, who stood with one hand drawn to her mouth, her eyes wide, cringing. Taggart stepped to her side and place an arm around her.

Fargo lowered his arms and unclenched his fists. "Either this clown is having a bad day," he said to Taggart, nodding to the unconscious hardcase, "or you need a better foreman."

Taggart's arm remained around Britt, possessively. He chuckled again through the smoke from his cheroot.

"As I was saying, Skye, I like your style. You're hired. You've got that job you came looking for. I can always use a man like you."

Several of the ranch hands came forward to lift Duff and remove him from the scene. The other spectators began ambling on about their business.

"Well, I could sure use the paycheck," said Fargo. "You've bought yourself a gun, Mr. Taggart."

He continued to avert his eyes from the blistering stare of the blonde. Britt stood there regarding him with loathing and disgust, now that she understood him to be one of them.

"You will have to work with Duff," Taggart added, with another bemused lifting of one eyebrow.

Fargo grunted. "He'll learn to like me if it kills him."

Taggart threw back his head at that, and emitted a raucous hoot. "There's a good one. You're sharp boy, yes you are. It'll be entertaining having you around, won't it, honey?" he asked of Britt.

She stared straight ahead, unresponsive.

Fargo noted an ugly bruise, partially visible on one of her arms. A few scratch marks were also apparent on each of her wrists.

"Well then, Mr. Taggart," he said. "I'll be reporting for work first thing in the morning. Much obliged."

He started to wheel the Ovaro about.

"Whoa there," said Taggart. "Hold on. Why don't you move in and get started here tonight?"

"It'll go easier between me and Duff if he's on his feet and has got his senses about him when I move my gear into the bunkhouse," said Fargo. "I'm not looking for trouble unless I'm being paid for it. I'd just as soon get along with those I'm working with."

The cheroot jutted from the corner of Taggart's smirking mouth. "A wise course. Better and better. Tomorrow it is, then. Be here at dawn."

"I'll be back," Fargo promised.

He rode off, throwing one glance over his shoulder.

He saw Britt being led into the house by Taggart, who tightly held her hand. But Fargo had the impression that Taggart was practically dragging her back into the house.

His final glimpse of Britt, before she disappeared into the house, was of her gaze following him. Her eyes ached with disappointment.

Fargo brought his eyes back to the trail ahead.

Taggart stepped down from the porch a few minutes later.

Duff stood in the ranch yard, looking off down the trail in the direction taken by Skye.

Taggart joined him. He was smirking. He admired the back of his hand and nodded back to the house.

"Nothing like slapping a bitch. Makes me feel good. I like the look on their face when they know you're going to hit 'em, and I like the way they beg you to stop." He worked up a snort of phlegm and spat it at the ground.

Duff kept staring at the trail as if he could still see the rider who had just departed.

"I want to kill him real bad, Mr. Taggart."

Taggart eyed him sternly. "You cut that thought right out of your head."

Duff gave a sideways glance with eyes that were gray as slate.

"Mr. Taggart, I wish you wouldn't have dressed me down like that in front of him and your woman and the hands and all. I only said what I thought you wanted done. I'm going to piss on that son of a bitch after I kill him."

Taggart drew a cheroot from his breast pocket. He lighted it, cupped against a breeze, and took several puffs.

"Duff, you're a heartless, mean-ass son of a bitch. That's why I pay you top dollar. Best money you'll ever make in your life."

Duff's slate-gray eyes went flat. "I think I do my job pretty good to earn it."

"You do, so far. But we've got a big job coming up in the morning."

"I know that," said Duff irritably. "The boys will be riding in from their day's work anytime now. I'm fixing to tell them over the fire tonight, while we're eating grub."

"Good. I want a report afterward."

"You'll get it." Duff's eyes went back to the trail. "So what about killing that son of a bitch?"

"That's what I'm trying to tell you. You settle your score with the new man later, and on your own time. And if I were you, I'd pick some other way to die. But for now, with what we've got in score for tomorrow morning, you'll do as I say, and I say we could have use for that man. He impresses me. We're going to take some losses tomorrow. I want that man on our side. When this is over, *then* you can do anything you want because I'll have what I want. I'll have it all. You forget about Skye for now. Just wait."

"Yes, sir."

Rowdy was a red haired, freckle-faced kid, barely eighteen. He'd been separated from his family two years earlier when the family was traveling west in a wagon train. This was a fairly common occurrence in the westward migration. In such circumstances, in the vastness of the West, family members were sometimes reunited, more often not. Rowdy gave up trying to find his people after six months, during which time he fell in with the rough-hewn men who worked the ranches several miles in either direction of the San Pedro.

The cowboys took Rowdy under their wing and he grew up tough fast, becoming a man while riding line, breaking broncs, even hunting buffalo one year when he was sixteen, when he and his outfit were cut off from the ranch by twenty miles of whiteout snowstorm that killed thirty head of cattle.

The kid got his name from scrapes in a string of cow towns: fisticuffs and a few shoot-outs where men went down. In Contention, Arizona Territory, Rowdy suffered insult from the Benteen brothers, and took on all three face to face over a shotglass of purposefully spilled whiskey. When the thunder rolled away and the smoke cleared, the barroom was smoky with the haze of burned gunpowder mingled with the overripe stench of freshly spilled blood. Two of the brothers were dead, and old Puff Benteen died the next afternoon from his gut-shot.

And yet, through this chain of violence, the sassy, smart-assed Rowdy never lost his open-faced affability. Everyone liked him. Rowdy had more salt than most, but he had a smile for everyone.

He rode into the ranch yard, to the stable. He stepped down from the saddle.

"Hey, Duff."

"Long day, kid?"

Around them, cowboys were occupied with unsaddling their horses. No one paid attention to their conversation.

Duff had been present when the kid took on and gunned down the Benteens. He was hiding for cover along with everyone else present, but he'd peered around an overturned table and had been amazed at how good Rowdy was.

Rowdy chuckled. "Long day, short pay." He started to unbridle his gun. "I need me a drink."

"Hold it a second," said Duff. "I've got work and we've got to head out now."

"Well, I guess so," said Rowdy, "but is it all right if I have that beer first, Mr. Duff?"

"It ain't all right." Duff's voice was taut, pitched low. "We're going to kill a man."

Rowdy's expression brightened.

"Well, hell, why didn't you say so? I'm with you. Let's ride!"

"I'll get my horse." Duff stalked off toward the stable. "Don't say nothing."

"I won't."

Duff was thinking, *The hell with Taggart.* What the boss didn't know wouldn't hurt him. But he would follow Taggart's advice and take along someone to back his play. With a straight shooting, piss-and-vinegar hellion like Rowdy backing him, Duff figured it was as good as done.

No one smart-mouthed him, as the stranger had, and lived.

No one.

The one who called himself Skye would be dead within twenty minutes.

Duff and Rowdy were positioned against the rise of a deep dry wash that had been carved by the elements through the eons into an otherwise flat, rocky landscape.

The wash cut deep enough for Duff and the kid to have tethered their horses to a juniper tree, below the line of vision of the man who rode into sight from the direction of the ranch.

Fargo rode at a steady gallop in the direction of Mescal, approaching them from about a quarter-mile away.

The trail cut south, in the direction of town. The middle length of the valley was an extended, sun-scorched prairie.

Duff and Rowdy had removed their hats, and were prone so that only their eyes and their rifle barrels peered over the lip of the wash.

"That's him," said Duff. He sighted along the barrel of a Henry.

Rowdy had himself a shiny new Sharps .50-caliber buffalo gun that he'd never used. That was the main reason he'd accompanied Duff. The world was full of low-down drifters, thought Rowdy. It wouldn't miss this one, if Duff had some reason for wanting a saddletramp bushwhacked. The Sharps could bring down a buffalo. He was itching to give it a try. But during the grueling ride here from the ranch, a disquieting unease had begun building in his gut, and he could no longer not voice it.

Even though the approaching rider was well beyond earshot, Rowdy whispered to Duff, "Are you sure Mr. Taggart knows about this? I don't want to get in trouble with him."

"Do as you're told and it will work out all around," said Duff. He never took his eyes from the man in buckskin astride the galloping Ovaro. He was speaking along the length of the Henry's barrel as it tracked Skye, who was now approaching a point abreast of them at a distance of perhaps yards. "Now do you feel like killing a man or not?"

Rowdy admired anew the line and design of his Sharps as he sighted the human target. He'd paid a month's wages for the rifle in Lordsburg a month earlier. So far he'd used it on nothing but stationary targets and some game. Nothing like this. Rowdy smiled. The sight centered on the rider, his finger curved around the trigger.

"So let's do it."

"On the count of three," said Duff.

After wending down the mountain slope, from the grasslands of the Taggart ranch, the trail had followed a roughly parallel course with railroad tracks off in the distance to the west, across barren emptiness. Bridges spanned the occasional wash. And there was a deep-cut wash, roughly parallel to the trail to the east as Fargo galloped along.

He'd been unable to shake the sour feeling of guilt whenever he thought of the disappointment in the woman's eyes as she'd watched him ride out of the ranch yard. Her face, her eyes, had not left his mind. He told himself that her disappointment in him would be temporary . . .

The Dragoon Mountains, to the east, were awash with the crimson of sunset. Those same slanting, final rays of the day's sun glinted off twin rifle barrels extending in his direction from the dry wash.

The Ovaro picked up their scent, dug hooves in, and reared its head, nostrils flaring a warning whinny.

"I see 'em," Fargo assured the horse.

He fell sideways, to sling himself so that he was hugging the side of his horse, away from the wash. Twin rifle reports cracked. The bullets whistled close enough overhead for Fargo to know that he would have been shot from the saddle, had he not executed this maneuver.

Hugging the side of the stallion, he unholstered his Colt, extended an arm so that the muzzle flash and report were as far from the Ovaro's head as possible, and pegged off two return shots. He steadied himself aright but stayed low in the saddle, and swung the horse toward the wash.

The Ovaro bolted him in that direction. Fargo held the reins in his left hand, the Colt in his right, holding his fire until he was sure of something to shoot at.

Another pair of rifleshots came from the wash. The shooters were now making no attempt to conceal themselves. Another pair of projectiles whistled too close for comfort over Fargo's head.

He urged the stallion on. The Ovaro ate up the distance to the wash, where a pair of figures scrambled for horses.

They'd never expected the man they were ambushing to hunt them down like an oncoming demon. They scrambled to mount up and spurred their horses, climbing the opposite bank of the wash, the horses' hooves kicking up a shower of gravel. Then they gained the flats and took off, each of them turning in the saddle, at full gallop, to snap off a shot from a handgun.

At this range, Fargo had nothing to worry about which is why he held his fire. He'd never before seen one of the bushwhackers, an energetic, grinning, hooting and hollering, redheaded kid in his teens, full of the devil as he rode and fired at Fargo, but he did recognize the other shooter riding hell-bent away.

Duff.

The Ovaro took the wash without hesitation, with one galloping, bounding leap. Fargo lost sight of them for a few seconds, then the Ovaro regained level ground, having gained on Duff and the other man.

The red-haired kid's horse suddenly somersaulted forward as if tripped by an invisible wire. The horse had tripped, breaking a leg in a prairie-dog hole, and the rider went flying, tossed to the ground.

Duff wheeled his horse and galloped over to help the kid onto his own horse. Then they continued on away from oncoming Fargo. But two men can never ride a horse faster than one. Duff urged the mount on cruelly with his spurs, while the kid turned and fired at Fargo.

Fargo rode in, remaining low in the saddle. He didn't hear this bullet pass, but he knew they were in range now and decided to try his own luck. His Colt roared as he rode.

The red-haired young man toppled sideways from the rear of Duff's horse and quickly regained his footing.

Duff shouted at the younger man, who was gripping his upper left shoulder.

Fargo couldn't hear what was being said for the galloping of his horse's hooves.

Duff looked in Fargo's direction, fired a shot that came nowhere near Fargo. Closing in, Fargo fired. His bullet went wild, too. Duff reined his mount around and rode out in a cloud of dust.

Fargo drew up before the kid.

The freckled face was grimacing, but though it would hurt like hell, the young man had sustained a nonfatal flesh wound to his left arm. Fargo noted that the kid's empty holster was belted low at his right hip.

A big pistol, a formidable Remington Army percussion, had landed several feet away.

The air spasmed with the pitiful cries from the horse with the broken leg.

Fargo looked after the receding figure of Duff, being swallowed up by the gathering gloom.

"What's your name, son?"

"They call me Rowdy."

"Yeah, I can see why. I don't much appreciate being shot at."

Every pitiable bleat of the horse made the young man wince visibly.

"Please, mister. Can I fetch my gun and put my horse out of his misery? He's been a mighty good horse."

Fargo nodded assent.

"Go ahead. Just don't do anything stupid."

"Thank you kindly."

Rowdy turned his back on Fargo and strode determinedly to the horse, not slowing as he stooped to retrieve his pistol. When he reached the horse, he promptly knelt, his back to Fargo.

There was a single shot.

Merciful silence returned, complete silence without even the crackle of night insects.

For several seconds, Rowdy remained kneeling. He would be saying parting words to the animal.

Fargo remained on his mount, observing. He'd holstered his Colt, but his hand remained on its grip. He didn't want trouble. But when Rowdy stood and turned to face him, Fargo didn't like what he saw.

Rowdy stood there, loose-gaited, knees bent, arms out from his side, his hogleg aimed at the ground. His eyes blazed, half calculating, half with wild abandon.

"Don't do it, Rowdy."

"I got to, mister. I ride for the brand."

"I can patch up that wound. I can give you a ride into town."

"You're not giving me nothing. I'm taking what I want."

The big revolver came up, fast.

Fargo drew faster. He squeezed off a single shot that took Rowdy high in the chest and dropped him backward so that he lay sprawled across his dead horse.

Fargo sighed. He holstered his Colt.

"You're taking a trip to hell, son. When you get there, tell the devil I said hello."

He thought about picking up the nice-looking Sharps the kid had dropped, but decided that doing so would lead to complications with Taggart. Let someone else get lucky finding the rifle.

He reined the Ovaro around in the direction of the trail leading to town.

9

Mescal was a small grouping of buildings—a hotel, saloon, restaurant, and a jail—practically at the foot of the twin massive water tank towers adjacent to the railroad tracks. Beyond were the stockyards, presently only at half capacity with cattle already sold, waiting to be shipped east by train. Temporary, shabby structures—some of them lean-to's, shanties, and tents—spread out in the opposite direction.

Fargo had worked up a hearty appetite, what with all the activity of the day, ending with the gun duel with Duff and Rowdy.

Fargo wondered what Duff would tell Taggart, and what would happen when Rowdy's body was found.

For now, though, Fargo's primary concern was that he was hungry enough to eat a chair leg.

He also arrived in Mescal with his course of action planned for the coming weekend. He would get Britt away from the Taggart ranch tonight.

Fargo had no intention of going to work for Cal Taggart. He'd have stood no chance of rescuing her in that yard, surrounded by Taggart's hands. And he'd have had no more chance if he had moved his gear into the bunkhouse on the spot, as Taggart suggested. He'd have placed himself in the constant company and under the close scrutiny of Taggart's men as any new man on a job, which would make doing anything impossible, given that he was so vastly outgunned.

He would let the ranch settle down for the night. This

would also allow him time to rustle up a meal. The grumbling of his stomach again reminded him that he'd eaten nothing but beef jerky since breakfast at the stage station. He needed nourishment for what he had in mind for tonight.

He also wanted to locate Jacob Jacoby's wife, to attend to the sad task of telling her that she was a widow.

Then, after midnight, when Taggart's defenses were down, he would return to the ranch and whisk the woman away. By this time tomorrow, the job would be done and Mandell would pay him the remainder of his fee.

As he rode into town, he noted the lack of activity. Those people he did observe in passing seemed to move like sleepwalkers, and he wondered why.

With night falling on a weekday, the streets of such a railroad cow town as Mescal, with its hard-working, up-with-the-sun populace, would naturally quiet down some around this time. But there was hardly anyone along the boardwalks of the downtown buildings adjacent to the water tanks. The saloon was closed, also an oddity this early in the evening in a working man's town.

Lights inside of the restaurant were on, though there were no horses or carriages in front of it. Fargo dismounted there. He looped the Ovaro's reins over the hitching post and walked inside.

A gaslight chandelier gave the restaurant's tastefully appointed interior a comfortable, warm ambiance, but the tables were all empty. Fargo closed the door behind him.

A moment after the sound of his entry, a woman appeared in an archway behind a counter. She had midnight-black hair and brown eyes. Her hair was pinned up, but he could tell that it would be full and flowing when let down. He also noted that, at five-foot-ten and about one hundred and fifteen pounds, she was a mighty fine-looking woman. She wore an apron over a gingham dress and was in the process of chewing a mouthful of food.

"I'm sorry," she said, swallowing. "I just sat down

back in the kitchen for a bite to eat. I should be up front here. I didn't think anyone would be coming in." She studied him, and he felt as if she were taking an assessment of him like he had of her, and that she, too, liked what she saw. She said, "You're not from around these parts, are you?"

"No, ma'am. Just rode in."

She seemed to make up her mind about something. "What's your name?"

"Skye."

"Hello, Skye. My name's Annie Mae Richards. There hasn't been a soul in here all day. I'm due to close now, anyway."

She walked past him and locked the front door. She turned a sign so that the CLOSED side was showing outward.

He started toward the door. "Didn't mean to put you out. I'll be going."

"Not at all. Tell you God's honest truth, I've got some celebrating to do and no one to do it with. Heck, I don't even have a dinner companion. I'm having some of my own stew and it's not half bad, if I do say so myself." She paused in the archway. She looked at him invitingly. "I like the way you look and I like your style. Care you join me, cowboy?"

Fargo strode forward with a grin. "I'd be right pleased to, ma'am."

Her high spirits were the perfect antidote to a day he wanted behind him. And she was a fine figure of a woman. The tender touch of a good woman could wash away the aftertaste of even the worst day.

The kitchen was well kept, clean, and homey. She motioned him to a chair at a small rough wood table, and went to the stove where she ladled stew into a bowl.

She set the bowl before him. "And stop calling me ma'am. I told you I had some celebrating to do, but I can't. Matter of fact, I feel guilty about feeling good."

He started eating.

The stew was awful. He chewed slowly.

"Mighty good stew, ma'am. I mean, Annie Mae." He

rewarded himself with a subtle glance at the attractive swell of her breasts from beneath the apron and gingham. He speared some potatoes with his fork. How could you go wrong with potatoes? He started chewing and soon found out. Pretending that the potatoes were delicious, he managed to say in a conversational voice, "So what are you celebrating?"

"I sold this place." She beamed. "Ever since I've opened it, business has been terrible."

He made himself swallow another mouthful. "No kidding?"

"No kidding." She enthusiastically finished off her bowl of stew, then dabbed at her lips with a napkin. Fargo noticed that there was a lushness to her lips, which were moist and looked kissable.

"A business man, riding the train from Chicago, stopped here just last week. He ordered the filet mignon. Except after he ordered it, he couldn't eat much of it because he said he'd forgotten that he had a stomach ailment or something."

Fargo forced down another mouthful. "No kidding," he said again.

"No kidding. But he said this location was so good, what with the train stopping for water twice a day and the town growing and all, that he thought he could really do well if he owned it. See, I inherited money from an uncle up north and I always thought it would be fun to cook. I never had to cook growing up, because we always had a maid."

"Uh-huh," Fargo said. He looked at the stew, wishing he did not have to eat any more.

Annie Mae stood and cleared her place at the table. "Anyway, one of his associates from Chicago is due in on the train tomorrow morning, and I already have my bags packed. They'll give me a check and I'll be gone from Mescal. I have enough to start over someplace else." She began idly rearranging things on the counter, her back to him. "I'm really happy to be heading out of here, tell you the truth. I wish I had someone to celebrate my good fortune with."

Fargo stopped considering his stew, and focused his attention on Annie Mae's shapely backside. He had been admiring her earthy beauty since he'd first set eyes on her. He rose from the table and crossed to where she stood. He knew enough about women to know that she was sending him a signal, inviting him back here into the kitchen and telling him this.

He took a chance that he was right, and slipped his arms around her, drawing her back to him.

Her well-rounded rump felt good as it pressed back against the front of his buckskin britches. He felt his member, separated from her flesh by but a few layers of clothing, rest naturally between the attractive globes of her hindquarters, and just as naturally begin to pulsate and grow hard. There was a heat from her flesh that he felt through the gingham and the buckskin.

He slid his hands up so that each cupped one of her breasts. His hands squeezed them and she moaned at his touch, tilting her head back, her hair tickling his nostrils. The scent of her—he wasn't sure if it was soap or her natural scent—was an intoxicating aphrodisiac. With one hand remaining at her breast, kneading its plumpness, coaxing its nipple into arousal, his other hand slid down to one of her well-shaped hips, the fingers of his hand closing over the fabric there.

Feeling impulsive, he thrust his hips forward.

There was a rattling as their bodies jarred the counter.

Steadying her with one hand to her breast, the other on her hip, his hardness throbbing through the fabric of her gingham-clad behind, he began a slow, primal grind.

She reared up and clasped his hands. Her moan this time was a feral growl. She pushed back and synchronized her pelvic movements to his rhythm and movement.

"Oh yes, Skye!"

Fargo moved a hand up so he could palm both breasts through the apron. He felt her nipples, erect and thrusting. He tweaked them with the thumb and index finger of each hand.

She sank back contentedly against him. "Oh my goodness. I feel like such a bad girl."

"You feel mighty good to me," he whispered, close to her ear.

The movement of her behind against his front told him she was far from finished.

He rotated her in his arms and again he felt the heat of her, even stronger now. Her breasts mashed against his chest. Her sparkling smile and eyes were inches from his face.

"Don't get the idea, Skye," she laughed, "that every cowboy who rides into town gets what you're getting."

Fargo chuckled. "Just the lucky ones?"

She bumped him a little with her elbow. "You're the first. Can't you tell how long it's been since I've had the touch of a man?"

"Well," Fargo reasoned, "no sense in stopping now."

Their lips clinched, fiery with hunger and darting tongues. His hands went down her sides to her rear. He cupped the delicious firmness of her rump.

"Oh, Skye, I want the real thing." She gasped like someone who was running. "Take me! Here! Now! Oh, honey, you do something to me. I need it so *bad*!"

"My pleasure."

They delved into another steamy kiss, during which he eased her toward the table. He intended to stretch her out on the table but . . .

She surprised him. There was no other word for it. He was in a class by himself at being the Trailsman in the wilderness, but in this world of sex, women never stopped surprising him. She straightened a leg, just as they reached the table, placed an ankle behind one of his ankles, and shoved.

Before he knew it, Fargo was flat on his back upon the table. For a moment it seemed as if she had disappeared. Then he realized that she had lowered herself at the table's edge, to work loose his manhood from the confines of his britches.

His erect rod sprang forth, quivering.

Annie Mae made a lip-smacking sound. "Dang, buster. Ain't you a good-lookin' boy? I haven't me one of these in too doggone long."

Before he could respond, Fargo felt that wonderful feeling of his member sliding into the warmth of her sucking mouth.

A minute later, just short of his exploding in her mouth, she stopped what she was doing, and stood between his parted legs. A few graceful movements and she was shedding the apron and the gingham.

Annie Mae was leggy and big-hipped. Her bountiful, beautiful breasts were capped with large brown aureoles that swayed as she climbed astride him.

Fargo noted, "You're not wearing any knickers."

"Never believed in 'em." She mounted Fargo, reaching down to guide his manhood into her. "All right now, cowboy," she said breathlessly. "Give me some of that good stuff."

"Yes, ma'am."

He grabbed her fine backside while alternately sucking her beautiful breasts. She shrieked and gasped and bucked as if she were riding a bucking bronco. Fargo heard Annie Mae make sounds he'd never heard from a woman before when she started to climax. He alternated steady rhythm with a halting, stop-go pace that elicited moan after moan from her.

When she was happily worn out, he swung her around so it was she who was pinned to the table, and he was standing at the table's edge. He flung one of her knees over each of his shoulders and started pumping anew. She surprised him by climaxing yet again when his own release bucked them together, coupling them as one.

10

Fargo and Annie sat at the rough wood table in the kitchen, holding hands like school kids, sipping coffee that was—praise the Lord, thought Fargo—far better than her stew.

As his world began returning to normal after the wildness of their lovemaking, Fargo found his mind beginning to work and analyze again. He waited for what he hoped was a suitable lapse of time before voicing what was on his mind.

"Uh, say, Annie Mae."

"Yes, Skye?"

"Uh, before we, uh . . ."

"Yes?"

"Well, before what just happened, uh, you told me what we're celebrating, but you said you felt guilty about celebrating."

She squeezed his hand across the table. This was obviously something she did not wish to discuss.

"Shucks, hon. I was mostly celebrating just meeting a nice fella like you."

"I've got business in these parts," he said. "It will help me get my job done right, maybe save my life, if I got the lay of the land."

She managed a maidenly blush. "I'd say you already got that, mister."

He extended his cup. "More coffee?" he requested.

"Sure, hon." She got up to pour him a cup.

He gave her rump an affectionate spank as she walked past. "You said you felt guilt about feeling happy," he reminded her.

"Well, let me ask you." She brought back the coffee-pot, poured him a cup, and he was pleasurably aware of the nearness of her bountiful breasts, again sheathed by gingham. She topped off her own cup, and returned the pot to the stove. "Skye, did you notice anything strange when you rode into Mescal?"

He leaned back in his chair, thoughtfully. "Now that you mention it, the town did seem kind of quiet, like a graveyard. Unusual for a saloon to be closed this early in the evening."

"The town's in mourning." She returned to the table. "That's why I said I felt guilty about feeling good. There's a dark cloud over this town."

"Who's being mourned?"

"A mother and her two small children. There was a terrible accident just yesterday. The stock pens were overfull. The train was late. There was a lightning storm in the afternoon."

Fargo grimaced. "That's a deadly combination."

"Sure was. Lightning spooked the cattle and because the pens were so full, they were able to bust loose and there was a stampede right down the middle of the street before anyone could do anything. It happened so fast. That poor Mrs. Jacoby and her children were just leaving the general store and crossing the street. They never had a chance. The three of them were trampled to death in that stampede. Two other folks were seriously injured, and one of them may still die."

Fargo paused, his coffee cup halfway to his mouth. He set the cup down. "Did you say Jacoby?"

Annie Mae nodded. "Sarah Jacoby. It's going to be a terribly sad day when her husband comes home. He's out prospecting."

"No, he's not."

Fargo told her about finding and burying the miner that morning. He chose not to tell her about Taggart and

Britt and his reason for being here. Annie Mae was on her way out of town, he reasoned. He did not want to place her in any sort of jeopardy.

Her eyes were sadder than before. "So tragic," she said in a small voice. "Mr. Jacoby died away from his wife and children, but it's as if this town killed their family; the greed and arrogance of men like Taggart and Yates. Yes, I'm glad I'm leaving."

"Who was responsible for the cattle pens being overcrowded?"

"The cattle belonged to Mr. Yates. It's happened before. Not a stampede, I mean, but Yates overstocking the pens. It was an accident waiting to occur. The railroad complained to him about it, the company from back East that owns the yard asked him to stop, but he wouldn't listen."

"Do the other townspeople feel the way you do?"

"Sure. But there's nothing anyone can do about it."

"Why not?"

"Because what Cal Taggart doesn't own in this town, Lew Yates does. A couple of heartless land barons, the both of them."

"Sounds like the makings of a range war."

"More than the makings," she said. "It's been heating up for a while. The two of them have bought off or run off everyone else. Now, Yates and Taggart want what each other has."

"Men like that never get enough," said Fargo. "It's a sickness in their soul. Sometimes they consume each other. I've seen it happen that way. What about the law?"

She made a face. "They're both above the law. They've each got themselves an army of imported gunhands." A thought occurred to her that made her scrutinize him across the table. "You're a man who can handle yourself," she said. "You're not in town to hire out to one of those two, are you?"

"Not quite."

She considered this, and when it became apparent that was the extent of his reply, she stood up and sashayed around the table. She settled herself on Fargo's lap, looping her arms around his neck.

"Well then," she said. "Now that we've gotten that out of the way, how's about a little more celebrating?"

The scent of her nearness aroused him again, and he felt himself growing hard. She would feel his throbbing erection between that sweet rump of hers, positioned so snugly on his lap. The scent of their lovemaking clung to her like an exotic perfume.

Fargo gave one of her shapely hips a loving pat, then rose to his feet, thereby making her stand, too. He willed his erection to subside and it obeyed, more or less.

"I'd love to spend more time with you, Annie Mae, if I could."

She stepped into his arms, not passionately but warmly and tenderly, with understanding eyes. "I know, Skye. And it does have something to do with Taggart or Yates, doesn't it? A man like you, well, if you're not here for them, you're here against them. It's one or the other."

He gave her a hug and they traded a kiss.

"The less you know about this, the better," he said.

"I guess it's good-bye, then." There was a tear in the corner of one of her eyes.

"I reckon it is," said Fargo. "Good luck to you, Annie Mae."

"And good luck to you, Skye. And thanks for two things. Thanks making me feel like a woman. I really have gone too long without. I'm choosy." She delivered a kiss to his mouth that tasted like honey. "I save myself for the best."

He felt oddly embarrassed. "Uh, you said there were two things you wanted to thank me for."

"Oh yes. Thank you for pretending to like my stew. That was very nice of you."

Fargo was at a loss for words.

"Now get on your way and get that job of yours done," urged Annie Mae. "But first, cowboy, take me in those arms and give me a hug and a kiss like we'll never see each other again."

Fargo was glad to oblige.

*   *   *

An hour later, moonlight provided illumination for Fargo as he cut away from the main trail about one mile short of Cal Taggart's range. The crisp night air awakened Fargo's senses, and the torrid interlude with Annie Mae had also served to revitalize him.

He'd expended considerable thought on her after they said their good-byes. He wouldn't have minded spending more time with Annie Mae, maybe even traveling north with her. But he banished such pleasant pipe dreams from his head. Doing so wasn't that difficult when he remembered the brutalized, dejected look in Britt's eyes when he'd ridden away from the Taggart ranch that afternoon. And there was a smoldering rage deep in his gut that hadn't been in him before, but it was now motivating him as much as his job for G.B. Mandell. Fargo's anger had to do with a young couple named Jacoby, and their children, coming west to seek their chance at an American dream only to be destroyed, chewed to a pulp by the evil of men like Yates and Taggart. Fargo felt an uneasy itch to do something about these two would-be Napoleons . . .

Even with the rock formations and curves in the terrain, he could plainly hear the large herd grazing on the range between the trail and the ranch house. It was a big herd. He'd passed it on the ride in that afternoon. He could now hear the clacking of the steers' long horns clipping each other, and the occasional, contented lowing.

He took care to circle the herd, keeping low in the saddle so as to provide less of a target in the moonlight to anyone perched nearby on sentry duty. But apparently Taggart had not placed any sort of security perimeter such as a floating crew of hands to patrol. Fargo was sure Taggart had the main trails carefully watched. But in Taggart's mind, who was there to challenge him? Any full-scale assault on his ranch would surely come with plenty of warning. Taggart had obviously never expected a lone man, quietly penetrating his defenses under cover of darkness.

At one point Fargo did catch a passing glimpse of the herd, over a ledge and down through some trees. A few cowboys here and there soothed the cattle with soft lullabies. No one down there saw the subtle shift of shadows on the ridge as the Ovaro, trotting as quietly as any Apache pony, carried its rider past.

Fargo dismounted within sight of the ranch house. He looped the Pinto's reins over a tree limb. He crouched in a copse of mesquite and surveyed the ranch house and its immediate surroundings.

The house, the yard, and the scattering of structures were clearly etched in the silvery moonlight. There was no one in sight, but despite the fact that this was a working ranch and it was past midnight, light shone from windows of the bunkhouse. As for the main house, there was a lighted window at the front, and a second light, obviously from the window of another room, at the rear. Otherwise, the house was dark. The effect was of two golden eyes peering at Fargo from the dark shape of the house.

He advanced on the ranch house, on the lighted window toward the front. He remembered hearing Taggart shouting to Duff that afternoon from that approximate vicinity. It would be, Fargo reasoned, the main parlor or a private office. He lifted a leg over the railing and crossed the porch on the soles of his feet, closing in on the amber rectangle of the shaded window without making a sound.

Men were conversing on the other side of the shade. The window had been opened at the bottom for night ventilation, and so Fargo could clearly hear Taggart and Duff talking.

"I don't like him," Duff was saying. "I don't like nothing about him, Mr. Taggart. It's a big mistake, taking him on, I'm telling you."

"Of course you'd say that," said Taggart. "He whipped your ass good today out in the yard. Don't you worry, Duff. He won't get your job. You've been my right-hand man for seven years. I put a lot of stock in that. I want you to keep an eye on him."

"Whatever you say, Mr. Taggart. Could I have another shot? This here is some mighty good whiskey."

"Help yourself to one more. Then I'm turning in."

"Yes, sir."

"But there's something else, Duff."

Fargo heard the clump of boots across the floor inside, and the clink of glass on glass.

"What's that?" asked Duff.

"I haven't seen Rowdy since he rode in. He's usually shooting the breeze with some of the hands around the yard after work."

Duff audibly slurped his liquor, then burped.

"I wouldn't know, Mr. Taggart. You know what a wild-assed, harebrained kid that Rowdy is. Good-natured as hell, but he's got himself a real knack for getting into jams."

"That's why I'm asking," said Taggart. "And I'm asking because he was seen riding off with you."

"Just doing our job," said Duff. "Some of the boys said they thought they saw some strays up on Crazy Woman Creek, but couldn't find them when they went looking. I had me an idea where those cows might be, and I took Rowdy with me in case I was right."

"Then I reckon I'm obliged to you," said Taggart.

"Not really, sir. Me and Rowdy, we went where I thought them cows might have gone, but there wasn't a sign of them and of course night was coming on. I headed back, but Rowdy said he had an Indian gal in those parts and he had a hankering to pay her a visit."

"As long as he's back for tomorrow's morning."

"Mr. Taggart, are you fixing for us to take that new man with us when we ride on the Yates ranch? You didn't say nothing about that to that fella, Skye. And me and the boys, we're all hot and ready to massacre every one of them mothers' sons come first light, just like you want."

"He'll ride with us," said Taggart. "And he'd better not catch a stray bullet in the head that's fired by you, Duff. I mean it. We can make good use of a man like that."

Fargo moved away from the window, uninterested in Duff's response. He'd already learned more than he'd expected from his brief eavesdropping. So Taggart's men were about to stage an all-out attack at dawn the following morning on the Yates ranch. Considering the tragic death of Mrs. Jacoby and her children, Fargo had little sympathy for Yates. He thought earlier than something should be done about men like Taggart and Yates, and it looked as if they were about to do it to each other! Good enough, in Fargo's opinion. All he really knew was that if Taggart was about to kick Duff out of the house, then the vital time was already tumbling away during which he could hope to accomplish his job here tonight.

He stayed close to the shadows of the house and made his way to the rear, where he was certain he would find the woman. It was certainly making the job easier, he told himself, with the mail-order bride herself wanting away from here. It was Fargo's experience that, too often, a woman involved meant complications. This was a nice change.

This window, like the other, was open an inch at the bottom, with a drawn shade. He heard no voices this time, but was sure that he detected movement inside. He decided to chance startling her. If he spoke to her from the porch he could be overheard by Taggart. Considering the bunkhouse full of gunhands, that would spell almost certain death if Fargo were discovered by Britt's window.

He eased up the window, brushed aside the shade and let himself in.

It was an oak-paneled bedroom without a trace of femininity.

Except, of course, for Britt.

She had seated herself on the double bed. She had been brushing her shimmering blond hair, but at his entrance, she leapt to her feet, facing him, her back to the wall. She wore a nightgown t t clung to the lush upthrust of her breasts. The filmy white material caressed her hips and seemed like a second skin down the length of her shapely legs. A silken print shawl was draped across her shoulders.

He tipped his hat. "Sorry to barge in on you like this, ma'am."

She stood there, staring wide-eyed. Her lips trembled, her eyes were pools of fright. She held the shawl tightly around her as a child would cling to a blanket for warmth.

"What do you want?" The whispered words were choked with fear.

He blinked in mild surprise.

"Matter of fact, I was under the impression this afternoon that you wished to be escorted off these premises. I am here for that purpose, and I suggest we move it right smart, if you please."

"But you work for . . ." Her voice faltered as if at the very thought of Taggart. ". . . you work for *him*."

"He *thinks* I work for him. Now come on. I've got a horse outside."

"No."

He blinked again. "Beg pardon, ma'am?"

"It's a trick. He's a sick, perverted bastard. He's paying you to do this, isn't he, to see what I'll do? Well, I'm not going anywhere with you. Now get out of here before I scream. I'd tell him that you went too far, that you tried to rape me. He'd kill you for that."

Fargo bit off a curse. He stepped forward her.

"Now listen, I'm taking you out of here if I have to throw you over my shoulder."

"*No!*" she cried.

She dodged away from him. The shawl slipped from her shoulders, revealing the lash-marks of a recent whipping. Fargo felt a flush of outrage consume him.

Britt's sudden movement knocked over a porcelain bowl and water pitcher from a dresser. The pottery hit the floor, and shattered noisily.

A shout was raised from the front of the house. Fargo recognized Taggart's voice.

Then he heard Duff shouting and cursing, then brusquely rousting the gunhands from the bunkhouse.

Running footfalls resounded as Taggart came charging

through the interior of the house, in the direction of this back bedroom.

Standing in the center of that bedroom, with the woman cringing in the corner, and the ranch yard erupting to life, Fargo unleathered his Colt.

Everything had gone to hell.

Now, it was kill or be killed.

11

Outside the bedroom window, with the night-shrouded ranch yard becoming more lively by the second, and with Taggart's footfalls pounding closer down the hall to the bedroom door with each heartbeat, Fargo hurried toward the window, pausing for one glance at the blonde, who had not moved from where she cowered.

He sensed that she was terrified to the marrow and feared the consequences no matter what the outcome.

"I came here to help you, and that's the truth," he told her. "I'll be back."

Drawing aside the shade, he stepped through the open window.

A different look had come into Britt's eyes, as if she almost wanted to go accompany him but could not summon the wherewithal to leave.

Then Taggart was at the other side of the door, vigorously rattling the door handle. Finding it locked, he hammered his fist on the door with almost enough strength to punch a hole through the wooden panel.

"Son of a bitch! What the hell's going on in there? Open the damn door!"

Fargo fired two rounds that were ear-splitting in the confines of the bedroom. Two large holes were blasted into the door at chest level.

He heard a mad scrambling noise from the hallway as Taggart, who must have been standing to the side of the door as a precaution, threw himself to the corridor floor, out of the line of fire.

Fargo flung himself from the window, out into the night. He landed in a smooth rolling motion and came to his feet where the shadows were inky black beyond the illumination of the window.

A pair of Taggart's cowhands came at a run around the corner the house. They practically collided with Fargo. They smelled of whiskey, and had drawn their handguns.

Fargo whipped his Colt around in a broad, swinging swipe. The barrel of the pistol slashed across their faces with enough impact to knock both cowboys to their knees, groaning and semiconscious. Fargo took off, sprinting in the direction of the tree line facing this side of the house, retracing his initial angle of approach.

He intended also to retrace his route of entry, in withdrawing from the yard, relying on stealth more than violence, hoping to avoid killing altogether though he remained ready to deal out lead if need be. As he sprinted for the trees, his Colt remained ready in his fist. His eyes scanned the night for danger, readjusting themselves in the dark night.

His reputation far and wide was that of a mankiller with few equals. The reputation was based on fact. What was not as often noted was that Fargo never killed ruthlessly, always preferring to use his brainpower over his firepower in confrontations. Sure, he enjoyed a good bare-knuckled tussle as much as the next man, but when he brought his hardware into play, he preferred the Henry or Colt to render an opponent unconscious rather than dead.

The pistol-whipped gunhands were left behind, and one of them was yowling in pain at where the Colt's gunsight had ripped flesh to the bone and also to alert Duff.

Ranch hands were running to the back of the house.

Fargo almost made it to the line of trees when someone opened fire.

Soon, projectiles whistled through the night. A couple of bullets drilled the nearest tree just as he left the moonlight and gained the deeper gloom of the forest.

His night vision was fully restored and guided him. The gunfire tapered off. He wondered if those near misses had been lucky shots, or if he'd been seen—in which case the ranch hands might be following in hot pursuit.

Fargo reached the spot where he'd left the Ovaro. His horse reared up onto its hind legs at the sight and scent of Fargo.

The abrupt movement startled the pair of gunhands standing a safe distance from the stallion, which had been snorting dangerously. They were savvy enough to know the Ovaro would only react this way to the presence of its master. They whirled about, their pistols already drawn.

"Damn me for a fool," one snarled to his partner. "I told you this horse belonged to that Skye fella."

They both swung their pistols on Fargo, the other snarling back, "Mr. Taggart is paying us to—"

The flash of gunfire from across the small clearing interrupted him. Fargo's bullet entered his opened mouth and blew out the back of the man's skull.

The second man opened fire at the muzzle flash, but by this time Fargo had repositioned himself. The bullet went wild. Fargo squeezed off a round that took this man in the heart, killing him instantly.

The Ovaro waited patiently for Fargo to step into the saddle. He wheeled the mount away. He urged the Ovaro into a gallop and found a narrow game trail that led downhill.

The stallion responded magnificently, negotiating the severe descent, knowing when to shift between oncoming trees and when to break into long strides across meadowland that became more and more predominant. As Fargo put more distance between himself and the clearing, Taggart's men would be gathering in the ranch yard.

The stallion beneath him was poetry in motion. The night became crisply cool, open solitude beneath a mantle of stars and moonlight that made everything visible and silvery. Then the Ovaro was retracing the circuitous route leading around the grazing herd that he'd passed on his way in.

He had almost, but not quite, relaxed when he happened on a pair of mounted cowboys who'd ridden up the trail at the sound of the gunfire.

They saw Fargo, and he saw them. Both of the cowboys opened fire.

The bullets came nowhere close to Fargo, but he reminded himself that they could get lucky. The Ovaro knew enough to take off galloping in the opposite direction. Rugged terrain soon stretched out between him and the cowboys. More shots were fired, one ricochet, then silence. Fargo rode on.

He doubted that they would follow him. Their job was to guard the herd. One cowboy would continue to tend to the herd. The other would ride back to the ranch to let Duff's boys know which way Fargo fled.

Skye rode around the grazeland, and before he reached the trail leading to Mescal, Fargo reined the Ovaro into an uphill climb, urging the horse up a steep rocky trail that seemed to climb to the moon.

The horse was sure-footed. Hooves clicked against stone like castanets.

There was no immediate hot pursuit by Taggart's riders, but they would be along sure enough, Fargo knew. But they would not be able to follow his trail across cold rock unless they had a tracker as skilled as he was, and Fargo doubted that.

When he reached the saddle of the crags overlooking the Taggart ranch in one direction and the lights of Mescal in the other, Fargo continued even higher, re-entering the pine forest on the opposite side, well removed from the Taggart ranch. He intended to make a cold camp, and consider what needed to be done. Taggart would have men out combing these hills for him, but this didn't concern him. He knew how to make a comfortable camp and not be detected by someone passing within twenty feet. And when tomorrow came, he would be rested and would have formulated a new plan.

As he rode through the darkness, he thought about a strategy to rescue Britt from Taggart. She would not be the first innocent young girl to think danger was fun until it got dangerous, as her life with Taggart obviously had become. But what began to trouble him was a dawning realization that he would be "rescuing" her from one man, doing so for money, so that he could deliver her into the waiting arms of another man, G.B. Mandell, who seemed to care more about his pride than about Britt.

He wondered if Mandell would welcome her with waiting arms, or talonlike clutches.

It was as if these men were dealing over a trophy, not a human being with a free will. He did not care for the suspicion beginning to gnaw at him.

He doubted that Britt knew he'd been sent by her mail-order groom-to-be. He wondered what she would say when she found out.

These were things to think on, because he was indeed working for the mining man from Silver City, and he was no closer to earning his retainer.

No one noticed when Duff cut away from the men he rode with. At least, no one called after him. They rode on while Duff followed a ravine jutting off from the trail. The hoofbeats of the others soon faded.

It was less than fifteen minutes since the fracas in the house had begun. Taggart's orders had been to fan out and canvass the area. Duff counted on his men assuming that he was pursuing some notion of his own.

The night was full of galloping hooves, the shouts of men, and the rattle of pistolfire, although no one seemed to be hitting anything.

He jerked his reins, and the dun he was riding drew up short at the base of a towering conifer. He heard approaching hoofbeats.

A rider passed, silhouetted starkly in the moonlight.

Duff recognized him. He saw the handsome stallion ridden by the buckskin-clad man named Skye. He held his breath as Skye rode past, far enough upwind along the rocky trail so that the Ovaro was unable to pick up the scent of Duff or his horse. Duff thought about unsheathing his rifle and popping the bastard, here and now, but decided against it. What if he missed? It would be a tricky enough shot from this angle. And if he missed, would he be able to elude a riled-up fella like that big, mean-looking bastard? Duff decided to stay where he was. He had his own reasons for being out here on his own, and no reason to offer up his life for Taggart's pay, alone, without anyone to back his play on a night-shrouded mountain. He would kill the buckskin-wearing bastard another day. Maybe tomorrow.

When Skye vanished from sight, Duff rode on. He had thought of the perfect way to cover his role in the death of Rowdy. Taggart would have his ass, sure enough, if he learned that a good hand had been lost because Duff had disobeyed direct orders and tried to ambush Skye. He rode hard and encountered no one.

He pulled in at the spot where he and Rowdy had ambushed Skye, or tried to. Rowdy's corpse remained near that of his horse. Duff broke off a long branch from a nearby tree, using the leafy branch to erase the tracks, every trace, of his horse's hoofprints in the dirt.

He retrieved the Sharps .50-caliber. Too bad, he thought. He wouldn't have minded keeping the rifle for his own. But of course it would need to be near wherever he left Rowdy's body to be found.

He stepped into the saddle and rode back in the direction of the ranch, staying to the trees.

He smiled. Taggart had liked Rowdy. Everyone had. Everyone would be riled as hell when they thought Skye had shot Rowdy tonight.

As he rode, Duff muttered aloud in the direction taken by Skye. "Enjoy your last night on earth, you bastard. Because tomorrow, you're dead."

In the bedroom, Britt had done her best to compose herself in the time since she'd been left alone by Taggart after the man named Skye had paid his unexpected visit.

After those shots aimed at Taggart through the door, Skye had flung himself through the window. Then Taggart booted the door open, busting the lock. Taggart stormed in breathing fire. Seeing the remains of the pottery upon the floor, he dashed instantly to the window.

But Skye was long gone, and Taggart had not even bothered to question Britt.

"I'll deal with you later," he snarled menacingly.

He'd stormed out and, with Duff, had mobilized the motley, half-drunk outfit to search the ranch, the trail to Mescal, and the high country.

She stood at the open bedroom window and overheard as they bellowed their orders. She winced when gunfire thundered so very nearby. Apparently the intruder had pistol-whipped two men just outside her window. After the gunfire died down, she concluded that Skye had gotten away. She wished now that she had gone with him.

She sat on the edge of the bed, brushing her flowing blond hair. *Damn,* she thought. *Damn!*

Taggart had placed a guard outside her door.

When he returned, she rose to face him. She held her back erect and forced herself to maintain eye contact with him.

Taggart kicked the door shut behind him.

"It's time me and you had a talk, blondie. I told you not to make me have to teach you again. You want another whipping?" He patted his belt buckle. "Are you trying to provoke me?"

"I did nothing wrong. You ordered me to stay in this room. A man broke in and I screamed for help. What am I to be punished for?"

"This man who broke in. Duff thinks it was the new man, Skye."

"It wasn't him." Emboldened by her lie, she thrust her chin forward. "You know who it was."

Taggart frowned. "What are you talking about?"

"This is all a big charade."

"A what?"

"An elaborate trick to see if I would try to run away. Well, I did as I was told."

"I'll believe you if you tell me one more time." Taggart glowered. "This someone who broke in here and tried to get you to leave, it wasn't that Skye fella?"

"It was not. I never saw the man before. I still don't believe that he wasn't sent by you."

Taggart snorted. "Don't act more stupid than you already are."

There came the clump of boots and spurs from the hall. Duff opened the door without knocking.

"Bad news, Mr. Taggart."

Taggart turned from Britt. "Let's hear it."

"The bastard killed Rowdy. They just found his body on the trail to Mescal."

Taggart's eyes darkened. "Damn. That boy had spirit."

"The boys tell me it looks like he put up a good fight. That Sharps was next to his body and it was fired, but he missed and that bastard got away."

"Hold on, Duff. Has anyone said they saw Skye tonight?"

Duff snorted. "The only ones who saw him tonight are dead. He's a mean-bred cuss, I'll give him that."

"That's why I want him on our side."

"But, Mr. Taggart, it don't figure any other way." Duff glanced at Britt. "We all heard her beg him to get her away from here. So tonight he shows up and tries to get her away."

Taggart patted his pockets, frowning when he realized that he was out of cheroots.

"Don't worry, we'll keep an eye on him. Right now, though, I'm going to saddle up. I want you to take me out to where they found Rowdy's body. Someone is going to pay." He turned on Britt. "As for you, you're off the hook for now, blondie. You keep on behaving, and you might have yourself a good life here." He turned to Duff. "All right, let's go."

They stomped out of the bedroom, allowing her a glimpse of the guard remaining in place outside the door. Then the damaged door was closed after them, and she was alone again.

She returned to the bed, brushing her hair, thinking.

There was no doubt in her mind now that she should have gone with the man named Skye. She brushed her hair with harder and faster strokes. *What a fool I am,* she thought miserably.

So much had happened since she'd witnessed Taggart shoot that hapless prospector. She'd become disoriented, afraid of her own shadow. Her stomach muscles cramped, bile rose in her throat when she remembered the horrific event. From then on, she'd felt nothing but loathing for Cal Taggart, and fear of him after the whipping he gave her. He'd spared her the buckle, which she knew could scar her for life. Her welts and bruises would heal. She saw no recourse but to adhere to his wishes, to his commands and demands. To survive, she would become his in this country where his word and will went unchallenged.

She'd thought she saw an opportunity for escape when the tall stranger in buckskins rode in that afternoon. This had earned her a slapping around from Taggart, who thereafter remained occupied first with what she interpreted as some important, secret event planned for the following morning, and then with Skye when he returned tonight.

Upon reflection, purely from the selfish point of view of her own survival, she thought that maybe it wasn't so bad, having refused to accompany Fargo. He'd been skillful and lucky to elude Taggart's riders tonight. Tomorrow would be another story. No one man could stand up to Taggart's private army, not even a fighting man like the tall stranger.

She finished brushing her hair. She blew out the kerosene lamp and prepared for bed.

She wondered who the man in buckskins was, really.

Britt fell asleep, smiling, feeling relatively safe in her warm bed and entertaining vaguely erotic notions about a man named Skye.

12

A muted gray slit opened the blackness of night along the eastern horizon to either side of, and behind, the mountains across the valley.

The moon had set, but a smattering of high clouds wafted by beneath the stars. The air was tart, nippy at this elevation, frosty even at this time of year.

Fargo woke an hour before dawn, as he had intended before he'd drifted off to sleep, after formulating his plan of action for this day. He had ingrained in himself the discipline of subconsciously allotting a set number of sleep hours before waking. When his eyes opened, he was alert as a cat startled from a nap. At such times as he could afford, he might allow himself to sleep for seven hours, though never more. More often than not, though, when on the trail and especially when on a job, he preferred to grab his sleep in four-hour increments, invariably finding this to be sufficient to replenish his spirit and strength.

Rising, he stretched, then he fed the Ovaro grain for breakfast. He washed down his own breakfast of hardtack with slurps from his canteen as he rapidly went about breaking camp, which this morning meant little more than rolling and tying up his bedroll. With his strategy formulated, there was no time this morning to find a flat rock, to sit and enjoy a cup of coffee and admire Mother Nature's handiwork with the coming sunrise, as he might otherwise be inclined to do. There would be no hot coffee because a fire would create a scent or smoke that would draw Taggart's trackers. He'd slept lightly, and neither he nor the Ovaro had heard or sensed riders passing nearby. He'd traveled uphill the extra distance and picked this spot, a rocky knoll overlooking the valley, because it was farther than a man, even a man on the run, would be expected to light out for.

Taggart and Duff would have their riders canvass the foothills and the trails in the mountains and in the valley leading from the Taggart ranchland, but there were no trails up this far.

Fargo saddled the stallion, then unslung the nosebag of grain. The horse would ordinarily whinny contentedly at that point, but kept quiet this morning, wise enough to comprehend these circumstances. His horse gave Fargo an affectionate nudge of appreciation. Fargo notched the grain sack and tied it behind the saddle under his bedroll.

He climbed into the saddle and rode back into the predawn gloom of the forest, where the starlight was blocked by high treetops. His gloved hands held the pommel and he spoke in low, encouraging tones to the Ovaro, giving the stallion mostly free rein to find its way down the treacherously steep mountainside. The horse slid and almost lost its balance several times on stretches of fallen pine needles. Each time, man and horse functioned as the single unit they had become. Fargo would lean this way or that, to allow his stallion to better maintain its balance. The Ovaro never hesitated in pushing on.

By the time he gained the rolling meadows and flats at the foot of the mountain, the silver slash to the east had widened to become an extended smudge beneath the purple mantle of starlit sky. Dawn was about forty-five minutes away, by Fargo's estimation.

He directed the Ovaro into a full-speed gallop.

The clustered lights of Mescal were beginning to flicker in the distance, off to his left, like waking firebugs. He gave the town a wide berth, rejoining the main trail that took him to the Yates ranch.

The plan he'd formulated for today hinged upon what

he'd overheard last night standing outside a window of the Taggart ranch house, listening in on the conversation between Taggart and Duff about a raid they intended for dawn this morning.

He arrived at the ranch in less time than he'd expected, which was to the good.

The brisk morning air and the physical exertion of riding hard across wide-open range had sharpened Fargo's senses. He was playing a dangerous hand. He hoped to stack the odds in his favor by catching those here as they were just waking up.

The layout of the ranch yard was much like Taggart's, the main house near a bunkhouse, stable, and corrals, with open range stretching beyond. Fargo had passed a sizeable herd on his way in.

Roosters were crowing, and so was a Chinese cook, clanging a metal triangle, yowling in broken English at sleepy-eyed cowpunchers, calling them to breakfast. Men moved about the yard in various degrees of alertness, some leading saddled horses, others walking to the stable or corral.

Fargo reined the Ovaro up before the front of the house just as a cowboy let himself out from the main doorway of the house.

The man started automatically toward the gathering of cowpunchers by the outdoor kitchen adjacent to the house. He was burly, and stood with an air of authority. He had foreman written all over him, thought Fargo. He wore a soft-collared shirt and chaps over his Levi's, with silver conchos decorating the front. He saw Fargo, paused, and watched Fargo dismount.

"Back in the saddle, pilgrim. We're plumb full up when it comes to punchers. Nothing for you here. You keep riding."

Fargo looked the man up and down.

"Seems to me folks around these parts could learn something about manners."

The foreman hitched up his belt. He wore a Navy Colt on his left hip, butt-forward.

"Is that right?"

"That's right. I rode out to the Taggart spread yesterday looking for work. They gave me a hard way to go, just like you're doing."

The man's brow furrowed. "You was at the Taggart ranch? Yesterday?"

"My friend, there's nothing wrong with your hearing. I spoke with Mr. Taggart."

Fargo glanced around at the gathering cowpunchers. They were a rough-hewn lot, similar to Taggart's riders. Most had a hand resting on the grip of a holstered revolver. *The two outfits were like mirror images of each other,* thought Fargo.

"The hell you say. You got some brass, stranger, coming from that den of snakes over here to our spread."

"I don't know what you're talking about. I know it's early, but I need to see Mr. Yates."

"Is that right? And how do I know that polecat Taggart didn't send you straight over here to plug Mr. Yates full of holes?"

"Tell Mr. Yates it's real important. Me and you are wasting time," said Fargo.

"Is that right?" The foreman lifted his voice and called, "Black Jim!"

There was movement from the gathering of cowboys. A man stepped into view.

He was a giant, well over six feet tall, whose physique, facial structure, and race made Fargo think of pictures he'd seen of African tribal chiefs.

The American West was a racial melting pot. The white man ruled through the overt brutality of racism, but the races did intermingle on a daily basis. Many blacks had escaped the South to travel west, and Fargo had encountered more than a few black cowboys.

Black Jim wore a dusty, battered cavalry hat, a red bandanna, and a lightweight pullover shirt and chaps. He wore bucket-top gloves, indicating that he was already saddled up and had been about to ride out.

He walked over, barely acknowledging Fargo with a

sideways glance, and said, "I'm here." His reply was in a husky baritone.

"I don't want to fight," said Fargo.

The foreman laughed. "Well now, that's just too damn bad." He said to the black man without taking his eyes from Fargo, "Jim, this here trail trash wants to see Mr. Yates. Says he's from the Taggart ranch."

Black Jim regarded Fargo for the first time with interest. He had a scarred, battered face.

"Is that right?"

"I said no such thing," said Fargo.

The black cowboy snorted. "Damn Taggart riders bushwhacked my brother. I swore then that I'd kill anybody from that ranch."

The foreman nodded. "That's why I called you over, Jim. Here's your chance."

Fargo said, "What I told your foreman is that they threw me off the Taggart ranch. I'm my own man."

The foreman sneered. "Tell you what, stranger. If you get past Black Jim here, and he's a mighty big if, then maybe I'll ask Mr. Yates if he wants to see you." He turned to the black man. "Jim, I want you to do your thing with this son of a bitch."

"Yes, sir, Mr. Childers."

The black behemoth started toward Fargo with measured strides, bringing up clenched fists the size of hamhocks. The knuckles were immense and thick with scars.

Black Jim had not specified whether the man killed was his brother by birth or by shared experience. At the moment, though, that didn't matter to Fargo as much as the determined hatred in the man's eyes.

Fargo brought up his fists, beginning to shift his weight loosely from side to side.

They squared off.

"Morning, Jim," said Fargo. "Kind of crazy, ain't it? I mean, you and me fighting and us not even knowing each other."

"Howdy," said the giant.

Then the hamhock-sized left fist snapped straight at Fargo's eyes.

Fargo ducked under it. "My friends call me Skye." He threw a straight left of his own that landed neatly but high on Black Jim's broad, battered face.

Jim seemed not to notice. "I ain't your friend." He came in at Fargo again behind another murderous straight left.

Again, Fargo sidestepped the punch. "Been working for Yates long?" he asked, just like two cowpokes passing the time of day.

"Long enough." Jim and Skye began to circle each other.

The onlooking cowboys were wagering on the outcome of the fight.

Childers watched with his arms crossed.

"Knock off the palavering, you two. I gave you a job to do, Jim. Do it."

"I been here long enough to know to do what Mr. Childers tells me," Jim told Fargo from behind his fists. "I do the dirty work, like killing off useless drifters like you, but I get paid, and good. I ain't no slave out here."

He came in and threw another long left.

This time Fargo was not able to dodge the blow. Jim nailed him hard on the jaw. Fargo's brain exploded with a flash like dynamite going off. But his instinct and skill combined to let him block a follow-through punch.

And they went at it, trading punches, bobbing, weaving, hammering each other about the head and body. Fargo regained a degree of clarity after taking the first punch. Each man gave as good as he got.

After a while, they each drew back to draw in gulps of breath.

Jim's face was bloodied, but he stood tall.

"You got me winded, I'll say that. I kind of hate to have to put you down, pilgrim."

"Likewise," said Fargo.

Jim leaped in with a lifting uppercut. Fargo weaved and blocked, and snapped out two hard right jabs to Jim's head. Jim swayed back on his heels, and Fargo landed a haymaker under the point of the big man's chin. Jim's knees buckled and he collapsed, unconscious.

Fargo took a deep breath. He drew the back of his hand across a cut he'd sustained beneath his right eye. The back of his hand came away dimpled with blood. But his senses were sharpening by the second.

The cowboys were settling up their wagers, grumbling among themselves. It seemed that most of the money had gone on Jim.

Fargo turned to face Childers and was not surprised to find himself staring down the barrel of Childers's pistol.

"Hold it right where you are, stranger," said Childers. "You're mean as a mountain lion, but I still don't know what to do with you."

"You said I could see Mr. Yates."

"I said maybe."

A voice said from the house doorway, "That's all right, Childers. Lower your weapon."

The man was in his middle forties, and he reminded Fargo of a toad; swarthy, slump-shouldered, no more than five-foot-two in height. He looked like a banker gone to seed. He wore a frock coat over a soiled shirt, with striped trousers and square-tipped boots. His oily black hair was thinning, and combed across his bald spot. There was a cluster of hairy moles over one of his bushy eyebrows.

Childers was eyeing Fargo as he would a dangerous beast, visibly reluctant to lower his revolver.

Fargo said, "You heard Mr. Yates." He paused for emphasis, adding ominously, "I don't much fancy having guns aimed at me."

When the foreman had reluctantly holstered his revolver, Fargo returned his attention to the man in the doorway. "Mr. Yates?"

"That I am, sir. I observed this bout of fisticuffs from the window. I must say, a most outstanding display of pugilism. Well done."

"We need to talk," said Fargo.

"I overheard you tell my boy Jim that your name is Skye."

"I just fought a *man* named Jim," said Fargo. "A hell of a man. And yeah, you heard right. Now do you want to hear what I have to say or not?"

"Very well," said Yates gruffly. "Come in."

Fargo glanced at the eastern horizon. Dawn was fast approaching, which meant that Taggart's riders were already en route for their raid on this ranch.

He walked past Childers, up the front steps, and across the porch. He could feel Childers's glowering hatred at his back every step of the way. Fargo thought of Duff, of his confrontation with the Taggart foreman yesterday. He decided that it would not be a bad thing if these two outfits wiped each other out. It was what they both deserved, as far as he could tell.

He drew up when another voice called to him.

"Hey, pilgrim."

He turned to see that Black Jim had regained consciousness and was getting to his feet. The ebony giant ambled forward, an arm extended for a handshake.

Their handshake was firm and brief.

Fargo said, "You pack a hell of a wallop with that left of yours."

Jim chuckled. "You scrap pretty good for a white boy."

Yates barked from the doorway. "Childers. Jim. Both of you boys get back to work. You," he directed at Fargo, "get in here. Let me hear what it is that you think is so all-fired important."

They entered the front parlor of the house.

A woman stood by the window where she must have observed, with Yates, the fight outside. She wore a faded crinoline dress. She was dark-haired, her hair worn in a tight bun. Observing her in profile as he entered the house and politely removing his hat, Fargo estimated her age to be about twenty, approximately half Yates's years. Her curvy figure caught Fargo's attention.

"Howdy, ma'am."

She turned slowly to face him. She had a day-old black eye, hideously puffy and purple. Her hands were clasped submissively before her. Her eyes watched the floor.

"How do you do, sir?" she said quietly, with a noticeable German accent.

Yates glared. "Shut the hell up," he snarled at her, "and get your fat ass back in the kitchen. We've got man-talk."

Her eyes never left the floor. "Yes, sir."

She left them.

Fargo watched her go, his thoughts were chilled by anger. He had never been able to abide the mistreatment of women.

After she left the room, he observed idly to Yates, "Quite a shiner."

Yates gave a man-to-man chuckle that made Fargo's skin crawl.

"You know how it is. She wouldn't pull my boots off fast enough last night, then started pouting when I barked at her to hurry it up some." He leered at Fargo. He punched one limp fist into his other palm. "Sometime you've got to beat a dog to make it mind."

"Sounded like she had a German accent."

"That's right." Yates snickered. "Hilde's one them mail-order brides."

"Is that right?"

"That's right. It's a good deal, I'll tell you."

"I'll bet."

"In Tucson and El Paso, they got bureaus that keep track of applicants, girls like Hilde from overseas who think they want the good life in America and they don't care who they end up with."

Fargo concentrated on the business at hand, but that subconscious gnawing returned. *Another mail-order bride. I'll be damned.*

"Can they get out of it if they want to?" he asked. "I mean, Hilde looks happy as can be. But I'm sure there must be some of those girls who decide they've made a mistake after they get here."

"You getting smart with me?" asked Yates. "Don't think just cause you whupped that big buck that I couldn't snap my fingers and have your worthless carcass filled with holes. You understand that, mister?"

"I'll mind my own business," said Fargo.

"Reckon I am giving you a hearing because of how you fought against my Jim."

"I've got a feeling Jim doesn't reckon he belongs to anybody but himself," said Fargo.

Yates appeared uncertain of what to say. Then he chuckled.

"You are a contrary bastard. Reckon that's just the nature of some men. As for Hilde, she ain't going nowhere unless it's over my dead body. She does what she's told and she's got a strong back, if you get my meaning. I told her if she ran away from me, I'd track her down and cut off one of her chubby little fingers. And I would, too. I heard tell Taggart got himself a mail-order bride, too. Taggart heard I had me a woman, and him and that rounder, Linder, headed up to the high country to bring him back someone to cook and keep his bed warm. See, mister, word travels fast on this range. Now why don't we get down to business?" He nodded to an archway. "We can sit down at the kitchen table and talk over some coffee."

"Right now," said Fargo, "you don't have the time for a cup of coffee."

Yates studied him sharply with glittering, toadlike eyes. "And why's that?"

Fargo glanced at the first light of dawn seeping through the curtained window. He'd purposefully taken his sweet time getting to the main reason for his being here. The longer he observed Yates, the more he felt the man deserved anything bad that happened to him, again making him equal to Taggart. Fargo had not come here to help Yates. He had come to advance his primary goal of rescuing a mail-order bride named Britt. And so far this morning, the timing for his formulated plan could not have been more perfect.

"You don't have time for a cup of coffee or anything else," Fargo told Yates. "That's what I came to tell you. Taggart, Duff, and their riders are on their way here right now. They intend to launch a full-scale assault to massacre you and your men within, oh, I'd say about five or ten minutes."

13

When Fargo delivered his news about an impending raid, Yates stepped back as if he'd been physically shoved.

"The hell you say!"

"I heard Taggart and Duff plotting it out."

Suspicion crept into Yates's eyes. "Tell me again why you rode all the way out here just to bring me this news."

"I didn't much care for the way they treated me over at Taggart's."

"They're barbaric bastards."

"Yeah, right," said Fargo. "I need a job. I figured this would help me get one."

He could tell that Yates's mind was processing everything. The rancher reached his decision.

"All right, saddle bum. Come with me." Yates stormed out to the front porch, shouting. "Childers! Round up every man here, pronto. And get your guns."

Fargo eased onto the porch. He held back and observed.

In the light of dawn, men scrambled and hurriedly assembled. There were fifteen of them, armed with everything from double-barreled shotguns to buffalo rifles to repeating rifles. Every man wore at least one sidearm.

Black Jim ambled up next to Childers. "What's the trouble, Mr. Yates?"

"Raiders coming," said Yates. "Taggart's outfit."

Childers eyed Fargo.

"Did he tell you that? How do we know he ain't in with them? How do we know he ain't playing some kind of trick on us?"

Jim snorted. "What the hell kind of trick would that be? We'd string him up alive, and he knows it."

Fargo eyed Childers. "If you don't believe me, believe your ears."

Before the foreman could respond, everyone heard the faint thunder of approaching hooves in the distance.

Childers gulped audibly. "Holy hell! Mr. Yates"— there was little enthusiasm in his voice—"you want us to mount up and ride out to meet them?"

Yates started to respond with authority, then faltered, wholly unsure of what to say. The rancher glanced at Fargo.

Fargo said, "You don't have time to mobilize and engage. You could fortify, and fast."

Yates's eyes shone with gratitude, and he whirled on the assemblage before him.

"You heard the man. I want men on every roof, and around every corner, ready for these bastards when they ride in. I want a man in every window."

Childers snarled at his men. "You heard Mr. Yates. Move, move, *move*!"

The cowpunchers dispersed with the sound of clinking spurs and rounds being chambered as men took up positions.

The foreman took cover with Jim. They concealed themselves at the corner of the stable. Childers held a repeating rifle. Jim held a Navy Colt in each hand.

On the porch of the house, Yates again turned to Fargo. "Uh, what about you and me?"

Fargo chuckled. "You mean, where would the safest place be?"

"Well, uh, yes, now that you mention it, of course. I mean, there is my wife to consider."

Fargo left the porch, unsheathed the Henry rifle from its scabbard, and led the Ovaro to a point of safety around the corner of the house.

"My guess," he said to Yates, "is that your sweet little Hilde sees trouble coming and has put herself somewhere well out of harm's way." Fargo stepped back onto the porch. "As for you and me, well I don't reckon there is a safe place anywhere on this ranch until after this fight is over."

The rapidly increasing thunder of hoofbeats seemed to be practically upon the ranch yard.

"Uh, right you are," said Yates, and he darted into the house.

Then riders were pouring into the yard from two separate directions simultaneously, charging down a hill from beyond the main house, and storming straight on in amid clouds of dust. There was shooting and gunfire.

Left alone on the porch, Fargo threw himself flat near the head of the steps, making as small a target of himself as possible. He heard bullets whistle past, splintering the wood of the doorframe behind him. He sighted the Henry on the closest horseman and squeezed off a shot—and watched the man drop from his horse.

He levered another round into the chamber and sought out another target, dropping a second horseman.

Then some of the riders saw his position and fired directly at him.

Fargo rolled behind the cover of the porch's knee-high wooden wall mounted atop a stone base. He stayed low. Bullets punched holes in the wood and ricocheted off the stone. He gained the far end of the stones and peered around the side.

The sound of breaking glass punctuated the gunfire as Yates's men broke out windows in their haste to get lines of fire on Taggart's raiders. A volley of gunfire poured into the yard from the house.

More riders dropped from their saddles.

The ranch yard was awash with billowing dust and the reddish-orange flaring of muzzle flashes. Amid the shouts of pain as heavy-caliber bullets drilled men came shouts of defiance from the riders who were pulling away to escape the gunfire from the house, riding beyond those lines of fire to continue attacking from other angles.

Fargo aimed the Henry and picked off a raider.

He levered another round into the chamber and was startled by an unusually loud *ka-thump*! He glanced that way.

A man was lying there, the side of his head blown away. Fargo moved to avoid the blood spreading out in a dark pool.

Behind Fargo, the dead raider had reached the porch; he had been about to shoot Fargo in the back when someone decided to take a hand in the matter.

Fargo looked across the yard. Through rays of the new day's sunlight shafting through the dust, he saw Jim.

The hulking figure of the black cowboy was clearly visible over by the stable, where he and Childers were making a stand, Childers firing rapidly with a rifle. Jim was firing away with a revolver in each hand. He and Childers were standing off Taggart riders who were closing in for the kill. Jim paused for only long enough to give Fargo a wave.

Fargo called over to him, "I owe you one, Jim."

Then Jim got busy again. One rider tried to run him down, charging straight at him. Jim swung up both his revolvers and triggered each, blowing the man from his saddle.

From the porch, Fargo sighted down the Henry and pulled off a round that dropped another rider who had been taking aim at Jim.

Jim's raucous laugh cut through the thunder of battle. "Much obliged, hoss. That makes us even."

Then he was exchanging fire with a pair of horsemen who were doing their best to outflank Jim.

Fargo picked off another Taggart rider. Fargo ducked as a bullet whined off a stone to his left. There was no way to tell who had fired that round. Bullets whistled everywhere. Fargo chambered another round, searching the yard for targets.

That's when he saw Duff.

Taggart's foreman was one of three riders advancing on Childers, trying to avoid the man's riflefire as he methodically chambered and fired round after round.

One of the horsemen dropped.

The clouds of dust and gunsmoke cleared briefly, enough for Fargo to see Duff exhorting his men to continue firing at Childers and Jim who remained back to back, fighting off the onslaught.

Childers's rifle jammed. He had been aiming at Duff and did not see another rider pulling down on him with a pistol. Childers only saw Duff's sneer. Childers threw away his jammed rifle and pawed for his pistol.

At that instant, Duff's horse was spooked by a nearby gunshot. The horse reared, and Duff became occupied with staying in the saddle and steadying his mount.

Fargo sighted and picked off the rider who was about to blow a hole in Childers's back.

Childers had his pistol halfway out of its holster when Duff steadied his horse, drawing a bead on him.

Fargo started to aim at Duff. Jim stood there like a bronzed giant, boots firmly planted, hollering like he was having the time of his life, twin revolvers spitting fire. Fargo became aware of movement to his left. Another Taggart gunhand was drawing a bead on him from the far end of the porch. Fargo swung the Henry and triggered a shot that blew away part of the porch, along with the man's face. Chambering another round, he brought the rifle around again on Duff.

But enough time had elapsed for Duff to fire his pistol once, twice, three times. The bullets took Childers in the chest, punching him to the ground.

Fargo took aim at Duff and fired. Duff's horse picked that instant to rear back again, and the bullet missed.

Movement to his right alerted Fargo. He tracked the Henry on a man climbing over one end of the porch railing for a shot at him. That's when he realized that the Henry was out of ammunition.

The gunman righted himself and swung his rifle in Fargo's direction.

Fargo let go of the Henry and threw himself into a prone position, unholstering and bringing up his Colt. The man fired and missed. Fargo triggered a bullet that sent the man flipping over the porch railing with a slug through the heart. Fargo then swiveled back toward the stable just in time to see Duff pump a bullet into Jim.

The bullet knocked Jim off his feet. It was a gut shot, and Jim wrapped himself into a fetal ball in agony, gripping his broad abdomen with both hands as if to stem the flow of blood bubbling between his fingers. He writhed in the dust.

Duff laughed cruelly. He pulled his horse over so that he was towering over Jim, and extending his pistol downward for the killing shot.

Fargo blew Duff out of the saddle with a .44-caliber round that pierced Duff's eye.

Fargo knew what he had to do. He had to get out there and drag Jim back to the relative safety of the porch. Jim was still thrashing on the ground. A gut shot was the worst way to go, the most painful, dying by inches; sometimes it took a day to die like that. Fargo had seen men in that condition pleading for a mercy round or for a weapon to administer a self-inflicted final wound. Jim was not making a sound. But he was alive.

The gunfire around them tapered off.

A Taggart rider shouted, "Damn, they got Duff!"

"Let's head out!" yelled another.

"Come on, boys!" shouted a third.

The handful of riders who had survived the defense of the Yates ranch reined their horses around and galloped back the way they had come, tossing parting shots over their shoulder through the dust.

Then they were gone.

The dust started to settle in the yard. Men started calling to each other. There were whoops of victory when they comprehended that the battle was over.

Fargo stepped off the porch, striding in the direction of where Jim had fallen. He felt no flush of victory. There was a bitter taste in his mouth, and he did not hurry.

Jim had stopped moving.

In a stand of trees about a quarter-mile uprange from the shoot-out, Cal Taggart and Tap Wiley sat astride their horses, observing the fight like generals commanding a battlefield.

Taggart lowered his binoculars when he saw Duff fall. "It's over," he said.

The badge on Wiley's vest gleamed in the morning sunshine.

"If you don't mind me saying so, Mr. Taggart, I think maybe I'd better vamoose back to town."

The sheriff was a stocky man in his mid-fifties. He wore homespun clothes, his white beard was scraggly stubble.

Taggart glared at him. "You're not afraid of being seen with me, are you, Tap?"

"No, of course not, Mr. Taggart. You know that."

Taggart looked downhill at the Yates ranch where he saw, even without his binoculars, that the remnants of his raiding party were turning tail under strong return fire from the ranch house and the stable.

"The boys know you're in my pocket, Tap. What's the problem?"

"Well, you know, Mr. Taggart, I am supposed to be a lawman even if I am on your payroll. What's happening down there, your men attacking Mr. Yates like that, why, that's illegal."

Taggart took his time lighting a cheroot. "So it is, Tap, so it is. All right, get your worthless ass back to town. And you keep an eye out for that fella who calls himself Skye."

"Maybe he's down yonder inside the house, or on the porch where we can't see him."

"Maybe. Or maybe he found out what's going on and is smart enough to stay out of it."

"Mr. Taggart, you seem kind of eager to want to trust that man."

"I'm no fool," said Taggart. "But if he is on the square, well, I want to know about it. I've got to replace Duff. I wanted you here, Tap, so you could see the power I've got. I've got gunslingers out riding line to replace the ones I just lost. This is a far sight from over. You keep an ear to the ground and let me know what you hear. And speaking of body parts, keep your nose clean, too. Anyone in town asks you anything about this, you say the dead men were part of an outlaw gang. You got that?"

"I got it," said Wiley, and he rode away.

Moments later, Taggart's riders galloped up to where their boss waited.

"They put up a hell of a fight," said one.

"Like they was waiting for us," said another.

"Mr. Taggart, they killed Duff."

"I saw it," said Taggart. "But I couldn't see who did it. Any of you boys see if it was that stranger calls himself Skye?"

There was a general shrugging of shoulders and shaking of heads.

"No way of telling," replied one.

"It was some hellion down on the porch," said another.

The men commenced reloading their weapons.

"I kept out of range of that one on the porch," one grumbled. "With the smoke and the bullets and all, I never did get a look at him."

Another voice chimed in. "Me neither."

"What we going to do now, Mr. Taggart?"

"We're heading out." Taggart cast a final glance down at the corpse-strewn ranch yard. "We'll leave Mr. Yates to clean up his mess. I've got the law on our side, and Yates has the message that I'm not a man to be trifled with. Let's ride."

14

Somewhere behind the ranch house, a wounded man was screaming in pain. There was the single blast of a shotgun, and the screaming stopped.

The peculiar, pervasive silence, always the immediate aftermath of violence, made birdsong, from a nearby tree, sound strident, discordant, and unpleasant.

The yard was strewn with bodies. Flies buzzed. Riderless horses wandered aimlessly, disoriented, bending down to nudge sprawled, inert bodies. To Fargo, it looked like the aftermath of a military battle.

He settled down onto one knee, next to the corpse of Jim.

The cowboy had died never having uttered a sound, but his ebony face was twisted into a hideous rictus of death.

Fargo sighed. He used a thumb and index finger to close the man's eyes.

These were tough men on both sides of this battle, who died hard, snarling at death. But there had been something about Jim. Fargo had found himself respecting and even liking the man during their brief acquaintance.

He stood to find the Ovaro coming over to him. Fargo greeted the stallion with warm words and a scruffing of the mane. He reloaded the Henry, replacing the rifle in its scabbard. Then he walked toward the house.

It was time to find Yates. Where the hell was he? The rancher had performed a vanishing act when the attack began.

About the yard, ranch hands were emerging from their positions in and around the house. There was much conversation as they reloaded, trading stories, tallying up losses against the number killed.

But no sign of Yates.

Fargo crossed the porch and entered the house. The interior was hazy with gunsmoke, with the smell of burnt gunpowder hanging over it all. Two men stepped past him, dragging out a body between them that left a blood slick on the wooden floor. Fargo went into the kitchen.

There seemed to be no one back here. The back door to the outside was closed and latched. There was a side room beyond a curtained archway, lined with shelves of canned goods and other household items. There was not much light.

He had to squint before he found what he was looking for, what would easily have escaped a hurried glance. He stepped through the curtained archway, and reached his fingertips down to trace the seam he'd discovered; a hairline cut in the wood of the floor.

"Relax, Mr. Yates." He spoke to the floor. "It's done. We drove them off."

He flipped open the hinged trapdoor and stepped back.

No one fired at him from down there. Yates's voice called, "Is that you, new man?"

"Yeah, it's me. You can come out now."

"Step forward. Show yourself." Yates's voice was breathy with near panic. "They could have a gun on you, making you say that. No one's blowing me to blazes today without meeting their own maker."

With his hand on his holstered Colt, Fargo stepped forward to peer down into the shallow crawl space that had been carved from the hard earth.

Yates crouched there, pointing a pistol up at Fargo. The German girl was down there with him. Yates's forearm was drawn across Hilde's throat, making a human shield of her.

Hilde was gasping for breath, tugging at his arm, trying

to release the pressure on her windpipe. She could hardly breathe.

Yates ignored her. "Are you sure we drove them off?"

"We?" Fargo repeated with mild sarcasm. "Yeah, we killed a passel of them and sent the rest packing." He extended a hand down to the woman, ignoring the pistol aimed at him. "Here, Mrs. Yates, take my hand. Allow me to assist you."

He maintained that posture for several seconds.

Yates emitted a long sigh. The rancher lowered his pistol and released Hilde.

"Good work, then," he said gruffly. "I figured my place was down here, protecting my wife."

"I see you did a good job of that," said Fargo.

Hilde took hold of his hand, her gaze connecting with Fargo's. He saw relief and gratitude in her eyes. And something else, which he could not define. He had never been very good at understanding women, much as he adored them. The young German woman came up out of the pit gracefully, her fingers feeling vibrant in his grasp. Then she released his hand and stepped through the archway.

He followed her into the kitchen, now sparkling in the sunshine pouring through the windows.

Yates followed them. He still held the revolver, his reptilian eyes darting here and there.

The sound of clumping boots and jangling spurs carried from the front of the hallway. Two cowboys were helping another man out of the house. This man was wounded, holding his bloodied side.

Yates holstered his pistol.

"Thunderation, what a fight. My thanks to you, stranger, for riding in with that warning so we could be ready for them."

"You lost Childers and Jim, and a couple more."

"Damn. That means I don't have a foreman, and that big buck was one of my best hands." Yates abruptly sent Hilde a withering glance. "What the hell are you gawking around for? Get out there in the parlor and start cleaning up the mess my boys left. Jump to it, now."

"Yes, sir," she said meekly.

She left them alone in the kitchen.

Yates stroked his weakly defined chin, turning to size up Fargo. "So your name is Skye. First name or a last name?"

"It's my name."

"All right. Fair enough. This isn't a country where a man should have to answer a lot of questions. A man should be judged by his actions."

Fargo's eyes were blue chips of ice. "Are you judging me? Am I supposed to care?"

"I appreciate you taking my side in this fight. You said when you rode in that you're looking for work. That's why I'm curious."

"Curious about what?"

"Well, reckon I'm curious to know how you came to find out that Taggart was going to have his riders attack me like they did."

"I told you," said Fargo. "I was at his ranch. I didn't like the way I was treated. Before I left, I heard Duff tell the hands about the plan. It was no big secret over there."

"And they just let you ride off with that kind of information under your hat?"

"I'm accustomed to doing as I wish. What's the matter, Yates? Don't you trust me?"

Yates made a placating gesture. "Skye, I'm asking these questions for a reason."

"It better be a good one. I just finished killing men who were intent on doing you harm."

Yates produced a handkerchief and dabbed at his sweaty forehead and balding pate. "I need a new foreman. Childers was a hardcase gunslinger who knew how to command. You possess those qualities."

"Yeah. But with Childers dead, that tells me it's a dangerous job."

"You're a dangerous man. I'll pay you two hundred a month and found."

"Found?"

"You'll get the lay of the land quick enough. I let some of the boys drive in steers of their own."

"You mean rustling." Fargo nodded. "You let your riders brand strays off Taggart's range."

Yates's toadlike eyes glittered. "You're mighty plain spoken."

"I like to know where I stand, and I like the other fella to know where he stands."

"Then we understand each other." Yates extended a hand. "Shake on it, Skye. You're my new foreman."

Fargo did not extend his hand.

"When do I start?"

Yates glanced down at his extended hand for an uncomfortable second, then dropped the arm to his side.

"How about you start this afternoon? I've got a job for you. Do I have your assurance of complete confidentiality?"

"Quit stalling and tell me what you want me to do."

Yates again dabbed at his perspiration then returned the handkerchief to an inside pocket of his frock coat.

"There's a cattle train due in Mescal, traveling east, at sunset. I've got one hundred head of cattle that I want on that train."

Fargo reached for a bowl of apples on the kitchen table. He chose one and took a bite.

"Seems like that herd should already be in the stockyard."

"I've had problems with the people in Mescal," said Yates. "They don't care much for me."

Fargo took another juicy chomp. "I heard about the stampede."

Yates growled. "What did you hear?"

"I heard about the lady and her two little kids getting trampled. Folks think it happened because you had those stock pens overfull."

"That's what I mean, them not liking me," Yates acknowledged. "And I don't trust them, either. So I'm pushing this herd in with just enough time to cut a deal with the man from back East. Then our part is done."

Fargo pretended to ponder this. "It's not a long drive. It could be done. You act like there's going to be trouble."

"There will be, if Taggart gets word what I'm up to. See, some of this herd, let's say there could arise a dispute of ownership." Yates's wink was intended to be cunning.

"In other words," Fargo rasped, "this is cattle that's been rustled from Taggart."

"Some. The point is, if Taggart finds out I'm driving this herd, he'll come for it."

"You mean," said Fargo in a neutral voice, "he'll try to rustle back his own cattle?"

A veil seemed to drop over the glitter in Yates's eyes.

"I'm not sure I cotton to the way you've always got a smart answer. If you're working for me, let's not forget who's paying the freight."

"Yeah, let's not forget that," said Fargo. "When do I see the color of your money?"

"When you come back from Mescal with payment for that herd. I'll pay you a month's wages in advance. See, cowboy, I've got money. Plenty of what they call resources. But I'm no shoot-'em-up type. I'm a businessman, know what I mean?"

Fargo nodded. "You don't like to get your hands dirty."

"There's that mouth again," said Yates. "But I reckon I'll learn to live with it if you get results. All you've got to do is see that what I want, gets done."

"Where's this herd you want me to take to town?"

"Grazing north of here at a place called Yavapai Springs. I got punchers there, ready to start them in on my say-so. Childers was going to take Jim and some of the boys and ride shotgun, you might say." Yates cocked his head, listening to the continuing activity from other parts of the house. Wounded men could be heard groaning and cursing amid muffled conversations and the sound of shattered glass being swept up. "Me," Yates concluded, "I'm going to assess the situation for my own self."

He exited the kitchen.

Fargo wanted to avoid the whole bunch of them. He started to reach for the latch of the door leading to the back yard. It was time to get away from here and implement the next phase of his plan.

He swung around, back into the kitchen, and drew up short, startled to see Hilde Yates standing directly behind him.

Fargo wasn't sure how she managed it, but the full-figured, little dark-haired German had drawn up closer on him than any adversary in battle ever had. Hilde's nicely rounded, plump breasts surged against the faded crinoline dress. *How the hell did she close in on me like that?* Fargo wondered. He could only assume that the fierce gun battle had dulled his senses, combined with this woman risking everything—a beating from Yates, at the very least—if caught back here alone with him, which gave Hilde ample reason for approaching him soundlessly.

He started to speak.

She bolted at him before he could, grasping one of his hands, yanking him after her, through the curtained arch. The unexpected jolt caused him to almost lose his balance, and he allowed himself to be led by her into the storeroom, his jaw gaping in surprise.

Inside the room, as he regained his balance, she leaned into him, tilting them both so that his back was to the wall, her plump, shapely figure pinning him there.

She reached one of her hands up to snake around his neck. She drew his startled face to hers. Her cheeks flushed with passion, she delivered a smoldering tongue kiss.

Fargo gulped for air. "Lady, I—"

"You can't imagine what it's like for me to be forced to sleep with a man who looks and feels like a toad!" she erupted. "*Herr* Skye, I have been violated by him often. It makes me feel dirty. It has been so long since I have been truly *loved*."

Summoning untapped reserves of willpower, Fargo reached down and took hold of her hand that had begun to engage in deliciously stroking him.

121

"Ma'am, I'm right sorry, and you can dang well believe *that*." He pitched his voice to a whisper. "And I'm sorry you've got yourself in this situation. I'll help you if I can."

"The hell with that," she rasped. "Help me with some hard and fast loving, right here, right now. I may never see you again!"

She began undoing the buttons of his britches. She licked her moist, glistening lips and looked up at him. "I need it," she whispered hoarsely.

He reached down to grip her by each wrist. He jerked her to her feet.

"I'm trying to tell you, lady," he whispered patiently, "I have a rule against getting involved with married women, no matter what the circumstance. It's just the smart thing to do."

"Please—"

She begged like a woman dying of thirst, pleading for water. Her bosom surged, erect nipples clearly visible, poking from beneath the material.

Fargo heard the clumping of boots from the hallway beyond the arch, approaching the kitchen.

He said, "Here comes your husband." He shoved her away forcefully. She stumbled back into deeper shadows. Without hesitating, he grabbed a loaf of wrapped bread, and stepped through the curtained archway, re-entering the kitchen just as Yates entered from the hallway. "Well, hey there, Mr. Yates. How do things look up front?"

Yates's toady eyes narrowed. "What the hell are you doing, still here? I thought I told you—"

"Not so fast," said Fargo. He crossed the kitchen to a cupboard. He looked inside, as if he owned the place, and brought down a covered bowl of dried fruit. He found some cured meat, and began building a sandwich. "I just took on this job. But there's a personal matter in Mescal that requires my attention first."

"Damnit, what about—"

"I'll be at Yavapai Springs by noon. We'll have your herd to the railhead when that train comes through."

"See that you do." Yates continued scrutinizing him.

"This business before you go to Yavapai Springs, does it have to do with Taggart?"

Fargo paused in making his sandwich. "I don't reckon that's any of your business."

Yates's eyes flittered to Fargo's low-slung Colt. "Uh, no, no, of course not!"

Fargo returned to the sandwich. "If it makes any difference, all that killing sort of gets a man's blood up, if you know what I mean. I've got a woman in town. I want to ride in and get some." He took a hearty bite of the sandwich. "That all right with you, Mr. Yates?"

He was banking on appealing to Yates's lascivious nature, and it paid off.

Yates leered. "Mister, I do believe you're my kind of man. All right, then. Go on and have your fun. But don't let me down, cowboy. You get that herd to that railhead on time. Me, I could use some attention from the missus. You seen that wife of mine about?"

"She was headed out back with the glass she'd swept up," said Fargo. "Said she'd be right back in to stay on the job."

Yates snickered. "She don't know how right she is."

He turned his back on Fargo and exited the kitchen. Soon his voice could be heard again from the front of the house, booming more orders to his men.

Fargo started for the back door.

Hilde appeared in the curtained archway, from the shadows. Her fever had passed, the surge of insane lust subsided. Her cheeks remained flushed, but she clasped her hands primly before her and looked downward like a penitent child.

"Thank you for not saying anything."

Fargo chuckled. "Hey, he might have gotten mad enough to kill us both. That's no way to get paid."

"You told me that you would help if you could."

"I will. But you're not leaving with me now."

"And why not?"

"You know why not. He'd have us hunted down within a mile of here. I'd be outnumbered, and we could both end up dead."

"But you said—"

"I'll do what I can," he promised. "Be careful, Mrs. Yates."

He chomped another bite from the sandwich and headed out, leaving her there. He found the Ovaro waiting for him. He fed the last portion of sandwich to the horse, then vaulted into the saddle.

As he rode off, he ruminated.

He supposed that no man could ever fully understand a woman. You could only do your best to appreciate, respect, and love them, to Fargo's way of thinking. And he would never understand the effect that he, a rambling rounder, had on women, while powerful, wealthy men like Yates and Taggart had to pay and threaten them for what was freely offered to Fargo on a regular basis.

He put such notions out of his head.

When he was beyond sight of the Yates ranch, he gave the Ovaro some heel. The stallion responded, lengthening out, stretching its strides, its mane flying. Short of town, Fargo cut off, retracing the route that would bypass Mescal and take him directly to the Taggart ranch.

15

Britt stood on the porch of the Taggart ranch house, watching Taggart address his cowboys. She appeared to be paying attention, but her mind was on the man called Skye.

Ever since their encounter the previous evening, when Skye made his surprise appearance and she'd resisted his rescue attempt—foolishly, she now realized—the handsome man in buckskins had been center-stage in her mind. Drifting off to sleep last night, her vivid dreams of him had been carnal; entertaining, arousing, however unbidden. This morning, she awoke and her first thought was of his safety.

What had become of him?

Would she see him again?

She snapped herself from this reverie when she heard Taggart's voice.

"So that's where we stand," he was saying to his men. "Now you know about the boys we lost, and how I'm upping your wages to make sure that you boys are riding for top dollar."

"You can count on us, Mr. Taggart," one hardcase called out.

Grunts of assent from the others.

"We're ready to ride when you tell us," said another.

And that's when Taggart said, "What about this Skye fella? Anyone seen sign of him since he rode out yesterday?"

"Here he comes now," someone announced.

Britt's gaze, along with everyone else's, swept to the man in buckskins who rode in at a gallop, reining up to dismount even before his stallion came to a complete stop.

The horse was lathered, and Skye wore a sheen of sweat. There was a sense of urgency about him, Britt noted, as he strode up to Taggart.

An unlit cheroot jutted from the corner of Taggart's tight mouth. "You've got some explaining to do, mister."

"I didn't come here to explain," said Fargo. "What's the big deal?"

"Bit deal?" Taggart chewed on the unlit cheroot, making it bob from the corner of his mouth as he spoke. "Somebody was around here last night and killed some of my boys. This morning we tangled with Yates, and it was like he knew we were coming. So before I hear you say anything, cowpoke, I want to know where you've been and I want to know what you've been up to since you rode out of here yesterday."

"All right, if it means getting the job done. See, there's a lady in Mescal."

A jealous female voice snapped from the porch, "I bet I know who it was, too. It's that trollop I've heard you men talk about since I got here, the one who ran the café, and who left on the train this morning."

Britt's shoulder-length blond hair shimmered radiantly, even in the cool shade of the porch. The starkly plain gingham dress she wore could not conceal her lush curves. She was pouting severely.

Taggart was snickering. "Now don't go believing in rumors, hon. That ain't nice. Annie Mae was a fine-looking gal, but she wouldn't give it up for anyone I know." He studied Fargo keenly. "That is until last night. What is it you got that the women like so much, Skye?"

"Well hell," said Fargo, scratching the back of his neck and temporarily not knowing what to say.

On the porch, Britt continued spewing at him.

"I don't care what they say. From what I've heard since I've been here, Annie Mae is just the sort of easy gal that would appeal to a no-account cowpoke."

"Ma'am," said Fargo, "as a gentleman, I feel that I've discussed the matter sufficiently in public."

She harrumphed. "Gentleman." She swung about and retreated into the house.

Fargo went from scratching his neck to irritably tugging at an earlobe. He was perplexed. He hoped she was acting, so as to conceal from Taggart their involvement with each other. But her jealousy sounded genuine. And her reaction last night when he had gone to her room to rescue her was proof enough that she was a wild card. He shunted these ideas from his mind.

Taggart was still snickering. "You handled that right smart," he told Fargo. Then his eyebrows drew together and his forehead furrowed. "Now let's me and you get down to business. When you rode in here yesterday and whupped Duff's ass, I hired you, as I recall. You were supposed to start today at dawn. Showing up late like this isn't exactly responsible behavior on your first day."

The ragged collection of hardcase cowboys loitered about, hands on their sidearms, listening in.

"It won't happen again," said Fargo. "She left on the train, like your wife said."

"Britt ain't my wife," said Taggart. "Yet."

"So what did I miss?"

"Not much, except that me and the boys rode against Yates. Duff got himself killed."

"That's a real shame."

"He didn't trust you, and I'm not sure I trust you, either," said Taggart. "I was counting on you to ride with us."

"I said it won't happen again. I've got something to tell you."

Taggart held up a hand. "In a minute. Did you tell Yates that we were coming for him?"

"How could I know that?" Fargo asked in a reasonable tone. "You didn't see fit to tell me, or I'd have made damn sure to be here. Now, do you want to hear what I've got to say or not?"

"Did you ride out to see Yates after you left here?"

"I'd already been to see him," said Fargo, "before I came here."

There was muttering from the cowboys. Several men cursed under their breath.

Taggart struck a match and got his cheroot going. "You've got grit, I'll say that for you. Now how the hell am I supposed to know if I can trust you? Why did you ride out to see Yates?"

"I was looking for a job."

"You asked him for a job? Then you rode over here, kicked Duff's ass, and got hired by me, is that what you're saying?"

"It is."

Taggart didn't seem to know whether to regard Fargo with respect, or as a crazy man. "Mister, what the hell were you thinking?"

"I wanted to find out which one of you two land barons paid the best wage."

"So I pay better than Yates, is that what you're saying?"

"It is."

Taggart looked at his men.

"You hear that, boys? You're riding for me, you're riding for the best pay on this range!"

There were whoops of rough-hewn camaraderie.

Fargo decided that this was the time to cinch his connection with Taggart. He said, "I've got my own reason for wanting Yates out of the picture."

Taggart cocked an eyebrow. "Oh really?"

Fargo nodded. "Ever get a look at that healthy-looking little wife of his? I wouldn't mind spending every night in bed with her."

Taggart laughed. "You're my kind of fella, that's for damn sure. All right, what is this news you're so all-fired eager to tell me?"

"I want a bonus," said Fargo. "Here it is. I didn't tell you yesterday because I had to think on it some. Yates wants me to push a herd of about a hundred steers to the cattle train that's coming through Mescal this afternoon."

The cheroot puffed from the corner of Taggart's mouth. "So Yates thinks you're working for him?"

"That's what he thinks."

"But you're really working for me?" Skepticism dripped from Taggart's tone.

"I told you that," said Fargo coolly, "and I told you why."

"Sure. Yates's woman, and a bonus. I know what you *said*. Now *prove* it. Where is this herd?"

"A place called Yavapai Springs. He boasted to me that some of the herd was rustled from you."

Taggart's mouth drew tight. "Well then, mister, I'm just going to have to rustle my cattle back, and the rest of that herd along with them." Taggart drew himself up straight. "There, you see? I can deal with that son of a bitch. Me and Yates, we're two of a kind."

"That's what I was thinking," said Fargo.

"Yates will want you to run that herd through a notch in the Mule Mountains, right before the trail opens up south to Mescal. He'll want you to cut wide around my spread, and that is the best route to drive that herd in time to connect with the train."

"I take it you know what you're talking about. This is your country. But we need a signal."

"Signal?"

"I've punched cows before," said Fargo. "Reckon I will again. This is a short drive, just a few miles from those springs into town if I hear you right."

"You do."

"Point is, more can go wrong in a couple of miles than on a long drive, and that looks to be the situation here."

"You watch for that notch in the mountains," said Taggart. He took a final draw on the cheroot and tossed it away. "If you're leaving Yavapai Springs before long, you'll push through that notch around four o'clock. There's a grove of pine trees and some rock formations up to the west as you travel through the notch. That's where I'll have my boys."

"Well and good," said Fargo, "but here's the deal.

This little hop, skip, and jump from the springs into town isn't going to be my last drive. I brought you this on a platter. In return, I call the shots."

"Is that right?" Taggart sneered. "And what exactly are you negotiating with, saddle bum?"

Fargo shrugged mildly. "The herd might not leave Yavapai Springs. Yates might reinforce his sentries. In other words, you might not get your hands on those cattle after all."

Taggart gestured to the hardcases, who had grown attentive.

"You'd double-cross me?"

There was a shifting of posture among the gunslingers, a narrowing of eyes. Hands remained on holstered pistols.

Fargo gripped the handle of his sidearm. "I don't much favor the odds, but I'll tell you what. Odds are one hundred percent that I'll drop you before your boys get me."

"Remind me again why we're standing here, fixing to blow holes in each other," snarled Taggart. "Damn but you are playing the angles. That could get a fella killed."

"That's what I'm trying to avoid," said Fargo. "I want to be gone from there before the lead starts flying. I'll stay with the herd until we get to that notch and that grove of pines you told me about. Then I'm riding away like the blazes. That's your signal. Then it's all yours. But I want to be out of there. When I ride off, that's the signal for your men to attack."

Taggart produced a fresh cheroot and lighted it. "Hell, that doesn't sound like much, considering what you're setting up. I appreciate what you're doing, by the way."

"That bonus will be thanks enough."

Taggart laughed. "You are a cold-hearted son of a bitch. Why does Yates trust you?"

"I impressed him, and he doesn't have a lot of choice. He lost a foreman this morning, too."

"Childers?" Taggart smiled. "Well, that's something, at least. And you being on the inside, with Yates thinking you're driving cattle for him, yeah, I like that." He eyed Fargo through a veil of exhaled smoke. "Just don't try anything funny, or you'll end up laughing facedown, shot full of holes."

Fargo swung into the saddle. "Have we got ourselves a deal?"

"We've got a deal."

"Adios, then. I'm off to Yavapai Springs."

Fargo reined the Ovaro about and rode at a canter from the yard.

Taggart glared after the receding figure. Then he said, under his breath so that only his cowboys heard, "It's going to be a real pleasure killing that son of a bitch."

"What gets me," said one gunslinger, "is that he got Annie Mae. Shoot. I've been trying for some of that for a half-year now and all I ever got from her was a smile."

As he rode away, Fargo vaguely heard their murmuring, inaudible conversation. He kept staring straight ahead.

He saw Britt in his peripheral vision. She stood on the porch at the side of the house, where Taggart and his men could not see her. She stood there with no readable expression, her hands remaining primly clasped before her. He felt her eyes on his back as he rode off.

When he had ridden far enough across sun-splashed rangeland to be certain that he was not being followed, Fargo left the main trail and let the Ovaro stretch into a gallop. He leaned low in the saddle, Apache-style, interested only in speed. The breeze felt good on his face and ruffling his hair. The sun was unpleasantly hot. The trail carried him higher, until he topped a rise.

And there it was, the vista of some one hundred head of cattle, bellowing, raising dust, stinking to high heaven, grazing around water that glistened in the sunshine.

He paused to take a sip from his canteen, then brought out a pair of binoculars from a saddlebag and surveyed the scene below. There were cowboys riding the fringes of the herd. He moved the binoculars until he spotted Yates, astride a gray at the center of a small group of his horsemen.

Everything was in place, thought Fargo, *in more ways than one.* It was time to implement the final phase of his plan.

His primary goal remained the return of Britt back to his client, G.B. Mandell. He'd tried the direct approach, had tried rescuing this "damsel in distress" last night at Taggart's ranch, and for his efforts had barely escaped with his life, empty-handed. His plan now was to play both factions, Taggart and Yates, against each other; to escalate their range war through off-stage manipulation and then pluck Britt from the ensuing chaos. He was confident that this strategy, playing both ends against the middle, would work.

Unless, of course, something unexpected happened.

He replaced the binoculars in the saddlebag, and rode down to meet Yates.

16

Yates greeted Fargo with suspicious eyes when Fargo rode up to the rancher and the hardcases who looked far more like gunslingers than cowpunchers.

"About time you got here." Yates, despite wearing a stylish tan duster worn over his frock coat, again reminded Fargo of a toad. "Damn, you ain't one for being early, are you?"

"I got up early enough to save your bacon this morning," said Fargo.

Yates conceded this with a shrug. "Yeah, I reckon. I thought maybe you wouldn't find your way up here, since I hadn't thought to give you directions."

"I can find my way anywhere," Fargo said, a mild statement of fact. "It's getting out of places that gives me problems more often than not."

Yates made a lewd, unpleasant sound. "The hell with it. Taggart may own the sheriff, but I got ears and eyes in Mescal, too. This hot gal you had to see when you rode out this morning . . . I heard she owned the restaurant in town. She left on the morning train with a mighty big smile on that pretty face of hers."

A nearby cowboy, overhearing this, said, "She sure enough was a fine-looking wench."

Yates leered at Fargo. "It was that girl who gave you the lay of the land, so to speak. That's how you found your way here."

"I don't discuss private matters in public," Fargo said.

Yates studied him through the dust stirred by countless

hooves of the herd that filtered the sunlight, making the air an unpleasant haze.

"I sure as hell wish I felt that I could trust you. There's something I don't like about you, Skye."

Fargo gestured to the herd. "Do you want me to move these cattle or not?"

Yates sighed. "Yeah, do it. Boys," he said to the nearby riders, "this is your new foreman, Childers's replacement. Goes by the name of Skye."

Fargo knew he must establish command here right off, and so he ignored individual acknowledgement of the cowboys. He said, "We're moving this herd out right now. If we run into any trouble, it will be at the notch before the trail opens up to Mescal."

Yates gave a low whistle. "You do know this country. You're right. If Taggart ambushes us, that's where he'd do it."

"Lucky for us, he doesn't know we're pushing the herd through," said Fargo. He turned authoritatively to the hardcases. "All right, break up this knitting bee and get to work. You men tell the others."

Except for one, the riders responded promptly, emitting enthusiastic shouts, wheeling their mounts to ride off, giving Fargo the impression that if anything, they were restless, more than ready to start.

The remaining rider stayed where he was, with both hands resting on the pommel of his saddle. He was lean, in his late thirties, Fargo judged, his red hair worn shaggy and a three-day stubble of beard covering his jaw. His holster was tied tightly to his thigh, gunfighter style. He wore a blue bib pullover shirt and Levi's, a short-brimmed Stetson and a large, bright red neckerchief.

"Well, Clay?" Yates asked him. "What is it?"

"I know who this man is."

"What the hell are you talking about?"

"This here is Skye Fargo. They call him the Trailsman."

Yates turned an uncertain glance on Fargo. "You said your name was Skye. Jesus, I wasn't paying attention. Skye Fargo!"

Clay made sure to keep both of his hands on the pommel, well shy of his gun. "I'm sure of it," he told Yates. He addressed Fargo. "I seen you kill three men in a bar brawl in Yuma. Last spring, it was."

"That was no brawl," said Fargo. "I was enjoying a drink and the companionship of a lady when they showed up in that bar, looking for me."

"The McWiggin boys," Clay recalled.

"I'd delivered their daddy to the state penitentiary that afternoon," said Fargo. "Those boys figured we had a score to settle."

"All three of them were carried out dead," Clay enthused. "They drew first, but two of them died with their guns only half out of their holsters. The oldest brother, he got off two shots before you drilled him through the heart. Yeah, I was there. I've never seen anything like it before or since!"

Yates waved a hand. "All right, all right. Enough." He was watching Fargo closely. "So what are you doing in these parts, Trailsman? What are you doing here, working for me, keeping who knows what other information close to your vest? I want an explanation."

Fargo decided that this would be a good time to flavor the deception with a portion of the truth.

"I've been hired to find someone."

Yates leaned forward in his saddle. "Who?"

"That blond foreign wench Taggart brought back from his trip north."

"What about her?"

"He stole her from someone else," said Fargo. "That someone has offered me money to bring her back."

"Does she want to go?"

"I don't see where that's any of your concern. But yeah, she wants out. Taggart's already slapping her around."

Yates's beady eyes grew introspective. "He's killed two women that way. Taggart likes it rough and the girls don't find out until it's too late."

"So you see why she wants out."

"You've still got explaining to do," Yates snarled.

"Why did you ride out this morning to warn me that Taggart's outfit was coming to attack?"

"A man's got to eat," said Fargo. "I can't do anything about the woman until after dark. Taggart's got too many gunhands for me to try anything in daylight."

"You weren't honest with me." Yates's tone was adamant. "You didn't let on to me who you really are, Skye Fargo."

"You're paying me to run a herd to Mescal," said Fargo, "not to recite my life story."

"I thought I was hiring a foreman."

"Who knows?" said Fargo. "I might like the work and stay on. I've punched cows for a living in my time. Nice thing about it is that the cattle don't shoot at you. I find it to be peaceful and relaxing work, a nice break from what I generally do."

"Which brings us back to Taggart's woman," said Yates. "All right, I'll buy that you're picking up extra money, running a herd like you're fixing to do for me. But I want to know about this morning, when you first rode in to warn me. Why did you do that? There's more to a man like you than just money, especially when a woman's involved."

Fargo thought, *And what the hell would a sidewinder like you know about a man like me?*

He said, "I thought I could use an ally against Taggart. That would be you."

Yates considered this. "And that's why you're here, driving this herd for me?"

"I'll make my move on Taggart tonight. In the meantime, why shouldn't I work for you?" said Fargo.

"You could have told me that you were Skye Fargo, for Chrissake. Do you think I'm fool?"

Fargo decided that it would be prudent not to respond directly to this question.

"Mr. Yates, if you do want me to run this herd to Mescal, palavering like this could cause us to miss that train."

"Very well," Yates growled. "Get started. I, uh, won't be going with you."

"Didn't reckon you would be."

Yates's toad-eyes glittered. "What the hell is that supposed to mean?"

"It means I knew what was going to happen," said Fargo. "That's a good thing."

Yates was caught unprepared. "I reckon."

"If I can figure out what's going to happen," said Fargo, "I can make plans to deal with it."

"Do you see anything happening on this drive?"

"No, not with Clay and his boys."

"Then get started," said Yates. "I'll be waiting for you at the ranch when you get back."

He wheeled his horse around and rode off. Fargo and Clay watched him go.

Clay's hands remained on the pommel of his saddle. "I sure didn't mean to make things dicey for you by popping off like that."

Fargo stood in his stirrups and extended a hand. "Shake hands, son. No hard feelings."

Clay sighed in relief, and shook hands with Fargo. "Much obliged, and I'll tell the truth. I've been wanting to shake your hand ever since that day in Yuma."

"Good to be working with you, Clay," said Fargo. "Yates is a spineless skunk, but that's got nothing to do with the fact that you ride for the brand. You knew something about me that you thought your boss should know, so you told him, not knowing what the consequences would be. You're all right, Clay."

"And you're right about that son of a bitch we're working for," said Clay. "I don't much care for the way I see him treating his own woman."

They brought their horses around and rode to the front of the herd.

Cowboys worked the outside, making plenty of noise, whooping and hollering, initially nudging some cattle with headbutts from their horses, the riders slapping at the steers' rumps with lariats.

The Ovaro picked up speed. Clay remained apace.

Fargo called over to him. "So why are you working here for Yates?"

"A man's got to eat."

Fargo winced at hearing his own words repeated. "Point taken."

"Something's been going on around here," said Clay. "Things really started happening when you showed up, but I mean even before that."

"What sort of things?"

"That's the blamed part I can't figure," said Clay. "I don't know, Mr. Fargo—"

"Call me Skye."

"Well, much obliged! I'd be proud to . . . Skye." The young cowboy beamed. "Anyway, it's nothing I can put my finger on. But Childers, he had me working a lot in the yard, breaking broncs in the corral, mostly. I ate my meals near the house. I guess it's just the way Mr. Yates and Childers been talking together, more than usual. They'd stop talking whenever someone like me came along, like they were planning something that they didn't want anybody to know about."

"Did anyone else say anything?"

"Sure. I mentioned it to a few of the boys and they said they'd noticed it, too. But then you showed up this morning and there was the shoot-out. Childers got killed, so I guess it doesn't matter."

The herd did not appreciate being driven away from the watering holes. The slowly moving mass of cattle made its sentiments known with unending, foghornlike lows. The clacking of horns, bumping into each other, was almost as loud.

Every trail drive that Fargo had ever been on had been longer than this one. He'd ridden the Chisolm Trail more than once, had done his time as a cowpoke, herding countless head of beef from the plains of Texas to the railheads at Ellsworth, Wichita, and Dodge, traveling through lightning storms that could startle a herd and turn it into an uncontrollable, rampaging mass of destruction. He'd fought Indians and raging rivers overflowing their banks when they were supposed to be dry and easily passable. It was a rough life, and this afternoon's trek was mild in comparison. But in one way, he reflected, every drive was alike, no matter the distance. Before long, a pervasive sense of monotony set in, plodding through the ceaseless dust, sweating from the grueling heat of a blazing sun.

The sun was arching into its westward descent when they reached the notch. The valley had gradually narrowed, its flanges funneling in to almost join where mostly barren hills were interrupted as if a break had been blown into a giant wall. The notch was less than a quarter-mile across. The herd already had its momentum and did not resist, guided by the horsemen into a narrower grouping as the men prepared to drive the herd through. Fargo glimpsed the vista that stretched out beyond and below the notch, the land flattening into wide-open prairie.

With Clay remaining at his side, Fargo reined in on a small rise that afforded a view of the surrounding scenery.

Redrock boulders had piled atop each other over the millennia and now bordered the cut in the mountains like towering sentinels. Saguaro cactus grew on the slopes above them.

"I don't see any pine trees," said Fargo.

Clay swabbed the sweat from his forehead with his oversized neckerchief. "You won't, either, and I ought to know."

"What do you mean?"

"I mean that there's some pine over near town and the ranches, but the elevation here is too low for pine. We've got cactus and scrub brush and mesquite."

"What do you mean, you ought to know?"

"I was born and raised in these parts," said Clay. "My family's ranch was one of them that Taggart bought out. It broke my daddy's heart. Mama passed of the consumption two years ago, and she's buried on that land. I've got happy memories of growing up there, from when Mama was alive and the ranch was doing good. But someone kept running off Daddy's cattle and burning our crops. Never did find out who, but I've got my suspicions."

"Taggart?"

The young cowboy gave a noncommittal shrug. "It was him who came around offering to buy the place. Times was tough, so Daddy took the offer even though my sister and me begged him not to. But that was the end of the family ranch. Sister is back in Illinois with one of our aunts. She's getting a good upbringing."

"And your father?"

Clay sighed. "He never got over what happened, losing Mama and the ranch. He gambled the money away. He was caught cheating at cards at a bordello in Tucson, and some men killed him."

"That explains why you're riding against Taggart, even if you have to ride for a scoundrel like Yates."

"I reckon it does."

Fargo continued to survey the slopes of the mountains. He remembered something Taggart had told him.

"So whoever told me that I'd find a grove of pine trees up here was lying."

"They were if they knew this country."

Cold apprehension snaked through Fargo, and he decided to give words to a thought that had been noodling around in his mind.

"Tell you what, kid. I'm fixing to light out from here right now, and I suggest you do the same."

Clay frowned. "Light out? You mean—"

"I mean hightail it."

Clay's eyebrows rose. "But that don't make sense, and it ain't right. What are you talking about?"

Fargo nodded in the direction of those riding with the herd, pushing it through the notch.

"These other men, are they from around here, too?"

"No, sir, not a one of them." Clay's eyes narrowed. "What's that got to do with anything?"

"Where are they from?"

Fargo continued eyeing their surroundings, intent on making his point so that he and the kid could get away from here. Even though he could not see trouble in the hills, he sensed it. He had a bad feeling. But having heard Clay's story, Fargo would not allow this hard luck kid to fall upon worse misfortune because of Fargo's actions, and it occurred to him that some of the others, despite their hardcase appearance, could have similar stories.

Clay shook his head. "Them are gunslingers that Mr. Yates hired from all over. He put out the word on how he was paying for cowpokes handy with a gun, and you know how word travels the trail. Fact of the matter, this country was a mighty nice place to live before the likes of Mr. Yates and Mr. Taggart moved in and brought these hardcases with them. There wasn't no killing and land-grabbing and hatred like there is now. Yes, sir, I wish times was like that again. But what do you mean about lighting out?"

"Just that. There's a lot going on that you don't know about, son, and I want you to have a chance because you deserve it." Fargo reined the Ovaro about in preparation for riding off. "There's no time, Clay. Take it or leave it. I say get while the getting's good."

Clay did not budge. "Now you hold on a minute there, stranger. The fact remains, Mr. Yates is paying me to do a job."

Fargo fought down a jolt of frustration. He held off pressing his knees to the Ovaro to signal withdrawal.

"Clay, listen to me. I'm talking to you straight. Loyalty is a fine quality in a man, but—"

Clay's head suddenly exploded, like dynamite set off inside a pumpkin, blowing the young man's head apart, fragmenting atop his shoulders. A rifle report rolled down from the hills, traveling an instant behind the bullet. By then, Clay's corpse was toppling from his saddle.

Fargo kneed the Ovaro and slapped the stallion's rump with an open palm for emphasis. The Ovaro bolted. A heavy projectile whistled less than six inches past Fargo's left ear. He leaned low against the horse, hearing the crack of the rifle. He glanced over his shoulder.

A wave of horsemen was descending upon the herd from behind both of the boulder formations bordering the notch through which the herd was passing. The horsemen roared downhill at the Yates men, their guns blazing.

A few cowboys caught bullets before they had a chance to react, shot from their saddle.

The cattle became spooked and rambunctious. The mooing and stomping of hooves became agitated, the herd picking up a forward momentum that soon had a life of its own. Fargo saw one cowboy get his horse butted out from under him by storming longhorns, then another. The cowboys fell screaming from view, to be ripped apart beneath the stampede.

The Taggart and Yates riders began firing at each other, dodging in and out amid dust and chaos as they swapped lead. Man after man on both sides was blown from his saddle by heavy-caliber bullets.

When he was well clear of that fray, Fargo reined in the Ovaro and swung the Henry from its scabbard, lever-actioning a round into the firing chamber.

A Taggart horseman who had been near one of the boulder formations, whose first round had killed Clay and been the signal to begin the attack, realized that one of the men he'd been firing at had outflanked him and was preparing to fire back. The man brought his horse around to make a run for it, to withdraw from the range of Fargo's Henry.

Fargo had liked Clay. There had been no reason for him to die. He sighted along the rifle barrel at the receding figure and said under his breath, "You killed the wrong one first." He squeezed the trigger, rode the recoil, and felt bitter satisfaction when he saw the rifleman drop from his saddle.

The short hairs at the nape of Fargo's neck started to curl. He chambered another round into the Henry and wheeled the Ovaro about.

Three men had ridden up behind him in the time it had taken him to shoot down Clay's killer. Cal Taggart was bookended by a pair of gunslicks, and each one of the three held a revolver aimed at Fargo.

An unlit cheroot bobbed from the corner of Taggart's mouth. "You didn't really think you were going to ride away from this, did you, hoss?"

Fargo froze with the Henry pointed skyward. He could

take one of them, maybe two. But he would be hit, and most likely killed. This seemed to be a good time to forestall getting killed, if possible.

"Howdy, Mr. Taggart."

"Drop the rifle," said Taggart.

Fargo let the Henry fall to the ground. "I reckon this means I'm not working for you anymore, is that it?"

"I'll tell you what this means," sneered Taggart. "It means you're dead. We're going to take our time killing you, you son of a bitch. And we're going to start right now."

17

"Dismount," said Taggart. "And drop your sidearm."

Fargo paused. This would leave him with his sheathed knife in his boot. It also left him more outgunned than he already was, and that much more at Taggart's mercy.

The shooting from the direction of the stampede, no more than an eighth of a mile away, continued. Wild-eyed steers thundered through the notch to disperse madly onto the prairie beyond. The popping of handguns sounded like firecrackers.

Fargo stepped down from the saddle, and gave the Ovaro's mane an affectionate scratch.

The stallion trotted a few feet off to the side and seemed to be observing the tableau, although this went unnoticed by Taggart and his men who had eyes only for Fargo, who now stood before them, his arms at his sides. Their revolvers were unwavering.

Taggart flicked a match and fired up his cheroot. "You going to drop that gun, or do you want us to kill you where you stand?"

Fargo unbuckled his gunbelt. He tossed the holstered Colt onto the ground near a clump of small boulders.

"You know, you're making a mistake."

The hardcases to either side of Taggart snickered.

Taggart sneered. "Do tell."

"It's a fact," said Fargo. "You tell a man you're going to kill him, that there's no room for negotiation, well, you've just told him that he's got nothing to lose. He might as well risk whatever he's got."

"Well, I'll tell you what, mister," snarled Taggart. "You've got nothing to risk. *Nada.*"

Fargo noticed, for the first time, the red droplets of blood across the back of his hand. He had been splashed with Clay's blood.

"I want to know something," he said. "That kid your sniper killed, the one I was talking to. His name was Clay."

Taggart held his cheroot between his fingers. He leaned over and spat. "What the hell about him?"

"I didn't even know his last name," said Fargo. "But then, I'd just met him. And there was that young cowpuncher of yours that I had to shoot down last night."

Taggart's eyes, through the smoke of the cheroot, became guarded, quizzical. "Rowdy. What about him?"

"And there was a man named Jim who rode for Yates. He died in that raid this morning. A lot of good blood has been spilled because of you and Yates. But it's Clay I'm curious about. He was born and raised around here."

Taggart snorted derisively. "And why am I supposed to give a tinker's damn about that?"

"He told me that he was raised on a ranch. Someone ruined his family, and then you came along and picked the ranch up for almost nothing. I was just wondering if you even know the names of the people you're destroying."

Taggart drew himself ramrod straight in the saddle. He threw away the cheroot. The knuckles of his fist whitened, holding the revolver he aimed at Fargo.

"I'll say this for you, mister. You've got some pair on you. Hell, I don't know the name of every person who's fallen on hard times around here."

"So why did you double-cross me?" Fargo nodded in the direction of the cattle that continued stampeding through the notch. "I delivered Yates's herd to you right on schedule. And if you wanted me dead, I'd already be dead. What about that?"

"Oh, I want you dead, don't you worry about that," said Taggart. "Everything started going bad when you turned up. That boy Rowdy and some of my other hands were killed after someone busted into my woman's bed-room last night. This morning, the raid on Yates went to hell. Duff thought it was because of you and in hind-sight I'm inclined to agree with him."

"It was a pleasure killing Duff," said Fargo, curious to see Taggart's reaction.

Taggart nodded impassively. "I knew it. You rode over to Yates and warned him that we were coming, then you fought against us. See, that's why I'm not killing you outright. I want to know why."

"Why what?"

"I want to know what the hell you're doing here, mis-ter, riding in and stirring up all this trouble. I want to know what you're about, to see if I've got to backtrack and cover my trail. I don't cotton to things happening that I don't understand. And I've got a hunch that you won't tell me if I ask you nice."

"Not a thing," agreed Fargo.

"What I thought," said Taggart. "That's why I'm not killing you right off. It's going to take some time to make you talk. You're tough. But you'll squeal like a pig when we get done with you. You'll tell me everything I want to know and you'll beg me to kill you."

"Don't count on it."

"And don't you overplay your hand." The rancher ges-tured with his pistol. "The hell with everything I just said. I'll drop you where you stand if you don't do what I say. Unsheathe that knife and drop it. Use two fingers of your left hand. *Now.*"

Fargo twisted a hand down, with a bend of the knees, to withdraw, with extreme speed, the wide-bladed knife that he always wore, sheathed in his boot. He must take out the two hardcases and then, somehow if at all possi-ble, he must take Taggart down without killing the man. With everything going on, Fargo's overriding objective remained the same even at a moment like this: the re-trieval of Britt and her return to G.B. Mandell. He took into account the possibility, however slight, that Taggart had moved Britt to another location since Fargo last saw her at Taggart's ranch. Fargo wanted confirmation from him of Britt's present whereabouts.

Fargo whistled. The Ovaro, standing obediently off to the side, had been forgotten by the horsemen. At Fargo's signal, the stallion knew what to do. The horse leaped at the nearest mounted man.

Fargo flung the Arkansas toothpick which sparkled as it sailed through the sunlight to embed itself to the hilt in one gunfighter's heart. The man fell from his saddle.

The other hardcase drew a bead on Fargo, but the Ovaro butted his horse, jarring him. His shot went wild.

Taggart fired, but had taken too long to aim.

Fargo dived for cover behind the boulders, pausing to retrieve his revolver as Taggart's bullet whistled by, uncomfortably close. He hunkered down behind the boulders, which were large enough to conceal him from the men firing at him. He caught movement from his peripheral vision and glanced sideways.

The Ovaro had trotted away from the horsemen, sensing that its task was complete, waiting now to carry Fargo out of this.

Taggart shouted to his man, "Get him, dammit! Get him!" He loosed several rounds that ricocheted off the boulders, then held his fire.

His man reined his horse into Fargo's view. The hardcase saw Fargo. His eyes widened, and he pulled his pistol around.

Fargo bolted directly at him, reaching the horseman before the man could aim. Fargo's left hand seized the wrist of the man's gun hand and twisted sharply.

The gunslinger cried out as his wrist snapped. The pistol dropped. The man cried out again when Fargo jerked, yanking him from the saddle, throwing him onto his back upon the ground.

Fargo was on him instantly, one knee pressing to the man's chest to pin him. Fargo leaned forward before the man could resist and placed his left palm across the eyes and forehead, slamming his head down against the ground. The man's mouth flew open to grunt in pain.

With his right hand, Fargo placed the large-bore Colt into the open mouth and pulled the trigger.

The top of the man's head ruptured, splattering a rectangular red smear across the ground. His struggling ceased.

Fargo darted back to cover of the boulders, sensing an aloneness that surrounded him. He peered past the boulder.

Taggart was riding away, hell-bent for leather.

Fargo retrieved his dropped gunbelt. The Ovaro trotted over before he completed buckling the belt back around his hips. He leaped into the saddle, and the stallion needed no urging to race off in pursuit.

Taggart was whipping his horse mercilessly. His escape options were limited. He could ride back the way the cattle had come from, but that led only into a winding trail to the foothills. He could not ride through the notch where the herd continued thundering through, where remnants of both the Taggart and Yates bands continued to exchange fire. It was his obvious intention to extricate himself from this shebang, and so it made perfect sense to Fargo when the rancher angled up the steep slope of the hill that formed this side of the notch. Taggart wanted to get over the hill and down the opposite slope, onto the flats where he could best put distance between himself and pursuit. As he rode, Taggart looked back and fired over his shoulder.

The bullets came nowhere near Fargo. The Ovaro was closing the distance on Taggart's mount, which was straining against the climb. The Ovaro cut the distance to less than twenty feet by the time they gained the summit.

Taggart's face was twisted almost beyond recognition by the exertion of riding, and with naked fear. In desperation, he flung his emptied pistol at Fargo. Again, he missed.

The Ovaro caught up with Taggart, putting Fargo neck and neck with him. Fargo jumped from atop his saddle and slammed into Taggart, sending them both flying to the ground.

Both men instantly regained their footing. Directly to

Fargo's right was a sheer drop-off from the summit of this hill to below, where great clouds of dust arose from the stampede. The tail end of the herd was just charging into the narrow cut, Fargo noted, and the gunfire from down there had tapered off. One way or another, the shoot-out between the gunfighters of the two ranches was over. Then he returned his complete attention on Taggart, who flung himself in with a swinging roundhouse right at Fargo's head. Fargo ducked under it and slammed a short, stiff jab, then another, to Taggart's side. Taggart made an *ooooof!* noise and collapsed to his knees.

Fargo stood over him, fists raised to rain down more punches. "That woman of yours," he said. "Where is she?"

Taggart remained slouched. He started to turn toward Fargo, his head hung down.

"What the hell does she have to do with anything?"

"Britt has everything to do with it," said Fargo. "You should have left her in Silver City. Where is she?"

"She's at the ranch." Taggart snarled. "Not that it will do you any good." He flung a handful of dirt into Fargo's face.

Fargo saw it coming. He raised an arm and blinked, which kept his vision clear. But then he was pitched backward, knocked off his feet, as Taggart followed through by launching himself at Fargo's knees. Fargo hit the ground.

Taggart was on him, a long-bladed knife drawn from his boot, coming at Fargo's throat.

Fargo used both hands to halt the hand plunging the knife. At the same time he drew up his knees and, using Taggart's own momentum, flung the man overhead, behind him. Then Fargo was back on his feet, whipping around to see Taggart stand.

Taggart bellowed, an inarticulate, primal roar, and flung himself at Fargo, still holding the knife.

Fargo shifted sideways, faster than Taggart could halt his forward rush. Fargo extended a foot and tripped Taggart, then used both hands to send Taggart pitching over the edge of the drop-off, into a free fall down to the dusty ground far below. Fargo turned and looked down.

The last of the herd was wending its way through the narrow notch in the land. There was no sign of horsemen from either faction. *Most of them are dead and the rest deserted,* thought Fargo. And there was no sign of Taggart. Fargo's view was obscured by dust.

The Ovaro again trotted over to him. He greeted the stallion with an affectionate touch of nonverbal gratitude. Taggart's horse was nowhere in sight. Fargo swung into the saddle. A few disoriented, wandering, riderless horses began to materialize through the slowly settling dust. He could still see no sign of the remains of Taggart, or of the other men he'd seen trampled by the cattle.

He brought the Ovaro around, away from the drop-off. He was thinking about one of the last things Clay had said before the kid got his head blown off; about something unusual brewing beneath the surface at the Yates ranch. Fargo had a hunch about what Yates was up to. And if he was right, there was no time to lose.

Fargo realized that delivering justice for what had befallen this valley had come to rest on his shoulders. He was the outsider. He had stage-managed and accelerated this range war to its ultimate, bloody conclusion for reasons of his own; rather, for one reason: Britt Lundgren. But now that he knew where Britt was, he would first take the time needed to continue setting things right.

He urged the Ovaro over the summit of the hill, cresting it, racing along the downward slope, toward the drab flatness of the prairie. He was taking the most direct route to Mescal, and if he were right, he would deliver more justice.

18

Fargo rode down the main street of Mescal.

Thin, scattered clouds above the mountains to the west had turned a striking reddish orange in color as the sun settled behind the mountains.

He rode past what had been Annie Mae's restaurant and saw a CLOSED sign in the darkened window. Thoughts of Annie's loving the previous night brought him a smile before he willed away that pleasant thought. He had not come to town this time for pleasure.

A few shabby businesses—a mercantile, the smithy, a gunsmith—were closing up shop for the evening. There was practically no one about. A line of horses was tethered in front of the saloon. Music from a maniacally happy player piano tinkled from behind the bat-wing doors.

Fargo continued on to the train station, which was across the tracks from the stockyard. An afternoon breeze dusted the prairie, and the cattle pens were presently empty, so the smell was not too bad.

The sound of a train whistle, like the call of some strange supernatural bird, lifted over the bleak prairie to echo back from the mountains.

Fargo dismounted at the station. He hitched a feedbag to the Ovaro, leaving the stallion to munch contentedly on some well-deserved nourishment. A plume of coal smoke snaked into the sky, and the whistle sounded again. Far down the railroad track, he saw the approaching train. He shifted his gaze to the station.

The luggage wagon was piled with freight and a mail-bag. Beside it stood the Chinese cook from the Yates ranch. The cook was staring off down the track at the advancing train, and so he did not see Fargo.

Fargo moved to the far end of the building. He stepped onto the platform and moved around to the front of the station.

With the approach of the train, people were emerging from the station onto the platform. There were about a dozen travelers in all, which made the platform somewhat crowded. The women held perfumed hankies to their nostrils against the faint odor of the stock pens.

A lawman stood leaning against the front wall of the station. He was stocky, unkempt, in his mid-fifties. His scraggly beard was white. His eyes were bloodshot. This would be Tap Wiley, the sheriff Lucius Brand had told Fargo about at the stage relay station earlier. It was the practice in towns like this for the local law to observe the comings and goings at stage stops and train stations.

Fargo passed Wiley, then drew up short when he saw who he was looking for at the far end of the platform.

Yates stood with his wife, Hilde, beside him, near where Fargo had seen the Yates cook. Yates wore his frock coat, a slouch hat, and striped trousers. He gripped a valise with his left hand, his wife's upper arm with his right.

His mail-order bride wore traveling clothes, fresh crinoline, and wore her dark hair in a severe bun. Her back was rigid. She radiated steely reserve.

Fargo thought of his encounter with her earlier this day, in the kitchen at the Yates ranch, and of how impossible it was to judge, from her outward appearance, the depths of passions she'd locked within her. He elbowed his way politely through the crowd without either Yates noting his approach from behind.

The train was about a half-mile off, the center of everyone's attention.

The cook was the first to see Fargo because of his position by the mail car wagon. Because of his race, he would be expected to ride in the mail car, not with the white folks. The cook saw Fargo and became so excited that, when he pointed, his excited exclamations were in Chinese.

Yates turned and his toady features darkened.

"You bastard," was his snarled greeting to Fargo. "I've been waiting here for you. You were supposed to be here an hour ago with that herd! What the hell happened?"

"You can forget the herd," said Fargo. "Taggart's men got us. They stampeded the herd. It's gone."

"Well I'll be go to hell."

"You told me you'd be waiting for me at your ranch after I sold the cattle," said Fargo. "You were planning to meet me here all the time. But that was supposed to be part of your little secret, wasn't it? You didn't mention that you were packing your wife and your cook and making a tactical withdrawal."

Yates glowered. "Didn't seem to be anyone's business."

Hilde held a purse by its strap before her, her eyes downcast. The brim of her bonnet made a shadow of the upper half of her face. Her expression was impossible to read.

"The word was out anyway on your plans," said Fargo, remembering what Clay had told him, which had helped Fargo draw the conclusions that brought him here. "Your ranch hands figured you and Childers had something brewing. He was going to come with you, is that it? When he got himself killed this morning, you knew for sure that you were losing your range war with Taggart. So here you are with a valise full of money, waiting on more money that you were going to make from the sale of that herd."

"The hell with that." Yates had to raise his voice to be heard above the chugging, clattering, and wheezing of the oncoming locomotive. "What about Taggart?"

"I think I killed him."

Yates snorted. "Well that's good news, at any rate."

"There's bad news, too, for you," said Fargo. "See, I may have to kill you next. I'd rather not, what with all these people about and everything."

With the sights and sounds of the train enveloping the scene, the bystanders were not paying attention to this conversation and could not overhear it.

Yates was standing close enough to hear Fargo just fine. "Why the hell would you be after me? I hired you, dammit. Was Taggart paying you?"

"I'm after you because you're half the problem of what's destroying this valley," said Fargo, "and since you're on your way out anyway, I'm making sure that you don't come back like you intend to after things settle down."

Yates snarled. "I have no idea what you're talking about."

"Didn't figure you would. Here it is, plain and simple. Yates, you're leaving this country and not coming back. I know people who will arrange to get a real lawman assigned to this town."

Tap Wiley appeared at Fargo's side, having observed the confrontation from across the platform and coming over.

"See here, what's going on?"

"I'll deal with you in a minute," said Fargo to Wiley. To Yates, he said, "You get yourself a horse and get the hell out of town."

Yates's narrow eyes blinked. "Horse? I don't need a horse. Me and my wife are taking this train, and I'll come back to my spread any damn time I want to."

"Hilde is taking the train," said Fargo. "You're riding a horse and you're not looking back, or I'll drop you where you stand. Is that clear enough? And you're leaving the valise."

Hilde's eyes snapped up from beneath the shadow of her bonnet. Her expression was keen with an emotion Fargo could not identify. She said nothing.

Yates drew the valise to his chest with both hands. "I'm not going anywhere without this. I'm carrying nearly all the cash I have in it."

Fargo glanced at the young woman. "Ma'am, do you want to be free of this man?"

Wiley harrumphed. "Now wait a second here!"

"Shut up, Sheriff," said Fargo. "I'm in the process of granting a divorce. Well, Hilde? Would you like to leave on the train, without this man but with the valise?"

She moved to stand beside him. There was no joy about her. Her plump cheeks were pale, her mouth was a thin, bloodless slash. She glared at Yates.

"I was lied to by everyone," she said, "beginning with the agency in my town in Germany. I hoped to better my station in life in your country with a fine gentleman." She spat at Yates. "He is no gentleman." Her eyes lowered. "He made me do . . . horrible, unspeakable things in his bed. He beat me, even when I obeyed. He is pure evil."

Fargo turned to Yates. "That means Mrs. Yates gets the assets of your marriage. That's my ruling. Yates, hand over the valise."

Yates took a step backward, clutching the valise, outrage and fear on his face, oblivious of everything including the deafening racket of the train pulling into the station.

"No! Take the bitch, but the money is *mine*!"

He stumbled back, tottering toward the edge of the platform. Another step and he would fall off the platform and onto the tracks, under the train's grinding steel wheels.

Fargo stepped forward. Instead of grabbing the man, he grasped the valise, and swung it sharply to the side.

Because Yates was holding onto the valise so tightly, he went swinging with it, releasing it with a startled shout only when his feet left the platform and he fell to the ground adjacent to the tracks, landing on his back, his frock coat flopping open so that a fat wallet went flying from an inside breast pocket. The wallet landed on the ground nearby. Yates wore a pistol in a belt holster beneath his coat. His eyes flared more like a cornered rat than a toad. He reached for the gun.

On the platform, Fargo set down the valise.

"I was afraid you'd do that," he said.

Wiley said, "Now wait one damn second!"

Yates had his pistol halfway out of his holster.

Fargo had been bluffing earlier about threatening to kill Yates, hoping instead that the bluff would avert gunplay here in a crowded setting where innocent bystanders could catch stray bullets. He now stepped off the platform, intending to disarm Yates with a kick to the jaw. He took only a half step from the platform, toward Yates, when a pistol shot barked from next to and slightly behind him.

Yates suddenly sported a third eye as a bullet punctured his forehead. He flopped back upon the ground.

Surprised, Fargo pivoted, preparing to draw his gun—this could be Taggart men showing up to even the score—but he froze, his hand on his Colt, his sidearm remaining holstered.

Hilde stood there, clasping a derringer with both hands. She had obviously drawn the gun from her purse. She dropped the pistol to the platform and stared at the corpse. Her eyes showed no emotion.

Wiley's eyes bulged. He reached for his gun.

"Holy mother of God! Now just hold on there, little lady, you're— "

Fargo turned and held the wrist of Wiley's gun hand, staying the man's revolver halfway from its holster.

"You hold on, Sheriff."

There was no longer the need to shout, since the train had completed rumbling to a stop. Its only sound now was wheezing steam.

Behind the engine and coal car was a trio of passenger cars, the mail car, and a string of cattle cars, stretching to the caboose. Passengers scurried aboard, and the windows of the passenger cars became filled with pressed, curious faces.

Tap Wiley puffed out his chest, reminding Fargo of an old rooster. "You let go of me, young fella. I'm discharging my duty."

With a flick of his hand, Fargo removed Wiley's sidearm from its holster. "You're not discharging anything, including this hog-leg." He tossed the long-barreled revolver to the ground. "Matter of fact," Fargo added, "as long as I'm discharging public duties, I think I'll discharge your services as sheriff of this community." He reached out and plucked the star from Wiley's vest.

This induced a smattering of applause from some of the onlookers.

Wiley's jaw dropped. "The hell you say. Mister, you're dead, I hope you know that. When Mr. Taggart finds out—"

"I just finished telling Yates," said Fargo. "Unless I'm mistaken, the only thing Taggart's finding out right now is how hot it is in hell. The point is, Tap, your services here are no longer required. Taggart is out of business." He cast a glance at the sprawled corpse. "And so is Yates."

Wiley managed to half close his gaping jaw. He pointed to Hilde, who stood unmoving, next to Fargo.

"But it's murder, what she did!"

"It was a public service," said Fargo. "Until some real law comes to this country, people have to administer their own. And some people are better off dead. How about you, Tap?"

Wiley's jaw dropped again. "Me?"

"You've got a choice to make," said Fargo. "You can go for that gun of yours over there on the ground. That won't end so good for you. Or you can get on a horse and ride out of Mescal and never come back. This is a day for new beginnings. I'd suggest that."

"Mister, what the hell gives you the authority—"

"I don't have the heart to shoot an old duffer like you," said Fargo, "and I've killed enough men for one day. I'll throw you in your own jail and wire for a real lawman. When he shows up, justice can take its course. Face it, Tap. You were fronting for a murderer and a thief. You had yourself a good berth, but the job's over."

Wiley sighed, and his bluster deflated as he exhaled. "I reckon you're right, if what you say is true."

"Believe it, Tap."

"Reckon I could live the good life down south. Frijoles. Whiskey. A young *senorita*. That'd do me for the rest of my days."

"Good choice," said Fargo. *"Adios."*

Wiley climbed into the saddle of a dun at a hitching post. He moved with the fresh-stepping gait of a man who had been liberated, not defeated. He rode off without looking back.

The ringing of a handheld bell broke the taut stillness.

A conductor called from the step of a passenger car, across the now-deserted platform. "Hate to break up the fun, folks, but this train runs on time. If anybody's fixing to get onboard, they'd better do it now."

Hilde remained standing at Fargo's side like a statue, staring at the man she had killed.

Fargo took her gently by her elbows and positioned her so that her eyes were looking into his.

She said, "I had to kill him."

"You heard what I told Wiley?"

"Yes."

"And about the money in the valise belonging to you?"

Her eyes clouded. "Yes." She nodded to indicate where Yates's overstuffed, oblong wallet lay near his body. "But that money should go to that man over there."

She used an extended arm to gesture her intention to the onlooking cook, conveying her intention for him to retrieve the wallet. Tentatively at first, and then briskly once committed to the action, the cook ran to pick up the wallet. He emptied the wallet of a wad of paper money, then tossed the wallet aside.

The train engine grated loudly to life, heaving, chugging, bellowing, and starting to move.

The conductor had studiously avoided looking in the direction of Yates's fallen body. He called out, almost cheerily, as if glad to be gone, "So long, folks."

Fargo picked up the valise and placed it in her hand. "Start a new life, Hilde. You deserve a second chance." He guided her, gently but sprightly, across the platform to the step of the car that was inching forward with an initial herky-jerky movement. He moved his hands to her fleshy, curvy hips and hefted her onto the step where the conductor's extended hand steadied her, pulling her aboard.

She retained her hold of the valise, and looked back at Fargo. He couldn't hear her above the locomotive noise, but he read her lips clearly through the steam as the train pulled away.

"Dankeschön." She remained, for an extra moment at the bottom step of the car entrance, so as to retain eye contact with him. "Thank you."

Then the cattle cars and caboose were rattling past him, picking up speed. The air became heavy with coal smoke and cinders, and the train was chugging down the track, away from Mescal, heading east.

He stood on the platform and watched the receding caboose.

"Good luck, kid," he said aloud.

Quiet descended. The breeze had died, and the bite of coal smoke was replaced with the vague stench of the cattle pens.

He returned to the Ovaro and removed its emptied grain bag, then took to the saddle. He felt satisfied with the completion of one matter. Yet his primary job would not be finished until he rode out to Cal Taggart's ranch one more time. He had seen to one mail-order bride. From this point on, Hilde's destiny was her own.

Which left remaining the woman that this was truly all about. It should have been cut-and-dried simple, but Fargo could not forget the way Britt had double-dealt him and nearly cost him his life when he had tried to rescue her last night from the ranch. Tonight, he would remain ready for anything.

Riding away from the station, he glanced back.

Singing happily, the cook was running off down the tracks in the opposite direction taken by the train.

19

Britt stood at the bedroom window of the Taggart house, watching the shadows lengthen across the deserted ranch yard. It became dark enough for her to see her reflection in the windowpane. She could see, in the face in the reflection, the indecision and worry she felt.

She was alone in the house.

Ordinarily, someone would have been left behind, assigned to keep an eye on her so she would not try to escape in Taggart's absence. Taggart expected to break her spirit in time, to wear her down, but for these first few days after having brought her here, he was all too aware of the free spirit that had sparked her to run off with him in the first place from Silver City. If he came back to the ranch and found her gone, he would have her tracked down and brought back, or killed. He had already physically abused her, and she had witnessed his senseless murder of that poor miner. He was capable of killing her, and going off to find another woman if she displeased him too much.

And so she remained at the ranch for hours after he rode off with his men that afternoon. That was the last she'd seen of any of them. She had not wasted her time.

Her blond hair was tied back beneath a flat-brimmed black hat. She wore a man's blue workshirt, a leather vest, a denim skirt, and riding boots. She'd packed a pair of saddlebags, one with grain, another with meat, bread, and dried fruit; what she needed to travel light and far. She intended to retrace the route they had taken south from the stage relay station where she and Taggart had stopped. The man and daughter who ran the station there were friendly, hospitable. She would catch a stage for the farthest point in whatever direction she decided upon between now and then. She had saddled her horse, which was waiting for her in the stable with a leather water sack strapped to the saddle. She had only to leave the house, cross the yard to the stable, and ride away.

Could she? *Would* she? The questions troubled her as she stood at the window, waiting, watching the gathering gloom.

And she thought of the tall, handsome stranger in buckskins who called himself Skye; not necessarily erotic thoughts, as those she'd lulled herself to sleep with last night, but now, as she prepared to make her bid for freedom, she realized that he was an unknown quantity. She could not be sure if, when, or where he would appear next. He had been the catalyst of much, if not everything that had happened since his arrival. He had a right to hate her, the way she raised the alarm last night when he came for her. Then, today, she had watched him ride out of the Taggart ranch yard and she knew he saw her, when her mind was thinking, *I'm sorry! Don't give up on me! Whoever you are, come back for me.* Was it foolishness to somehow think that she could make him hear what she was thinking?

Cal Taggart had been right to worry about keeping a constant eye on her, to distrust her. Her blood ran cold at the awareness of the hell she had been thrust into, seeking only fun and adventure in this exciting New World when she'd first left her home overseas. Perhaps, she had come to believe, everything that had happened since she'd pretended to be kidnapped in Silver City, every sad turn of her life since running off with Taggart, could have been atonement for having swindled G.B. Mandell out of the ransom he paid Taggart for her release. If so, then the slate was clean. She had been through hell at Taggart's hands, she had never seen a cent of the money, and her long-range future seemed that of a domesticated slave shackled by the fear of beatings and worse. Mandell had likewise proven to be a foul lecherous brute who made her cringe. On their first meeting, after he'd sent a coach for his mail-order bride in Silver City, not even deigning to come himself, his manner had been ungentlemanly, suggestive. Mandell's eyes had roamed the curves of her body and he had actually smacked his lips and touched his private parts through his slacks in her presence! This had been her introduction to her future husband. Repulsion, and her impulsive, lusty meeting of Taggart before the wedding to Mandell, had begun a spiraling chain of events. She had traded the security of her homeland, the comfortable life she'd known, for a savage land of random, deadly violence amid a medieval war between two evil kings, Yates and the man she had been foolish enough to become infatuated with, Taggart.

There was an eerie, desolate quiet to the ranch. Roosters made noise, calling their chickens to roost. A jackass brayed at the setting sun. Hours had passed without any sign of human activity.

With darkness falling, she knew that she must act.

Something was wrong. Wrong for Taggart. Right for her, and she could care less about the details. She knew only that he and his men had again ridden off against the Yates outfit after Skye's second visit. By now at least one Taggart man should have ridden back. Something had happened . . .

She snatched up the saddlebags and left the bedroom, determined not to get cold feet and decide to stay. She strode through the house, into the main foyer, wistfully partaking again of the elegance of the interior of Taggart's home. Although he said he had lived here alone, and though the furnishings were of the rough, polished hardwood of the Southwest, there was an artistic touch to the arrangement of the furniture and rugs, the placement of decorative cacti and plants, even draperies, making Britt think of a woman's touch contributing to this home . . . but when?

She left the house, crossed the porch and traversed the yard to the stable. She carried a Colt revolver in one of the saddlebags. She didn't want to ever use a gun to shoot anyone, and yet she knew she would need one in this harsh, deadly land.

There was within her a vague disappointment that Skye had not returned to help her, or to at least look in on her to see how she was doing. Yes, he had a right to hate her. That would explain why he had not ridden out here to the Taggart ranch one more time.

That was life. She would never see him again.

She reached the stable and stepped inside. Her horse heard her approach and whinnied, shuffling its hooves in the gloomy interior. A chill touched the base of her spine. The animal was not greeting her with anticipation, but with warning. She reached for the revolver in her saddlebag.

A hand darted out from the shadows to clench one of her wrists, and tugged brutally. She heard a voice that she recognized instantly.

Taggart snarled, "You *bitch*!"

She was thrown onto the ground. The saddlebags flew from her, beyond her reach. She twisted this way and that, and struggled to her feet.

Without releasing his viselike grip on her, Taggart appeared from where he had been waiting, stepping into the scant, grimy light of the stable.

She gasped at his appearance.

He bore scant resemblance to the dangerously debonair, cheroot-puffing gentleman rancher who had favored polished boots, pressed slacks and shirt, and a carefully blocked hat. At present, his clothes were soiled, in tattered disarray. His hair was mussed, his face bruised, coated with dust. His eyes burned with savage madness.

"Cal," she said, regaining her footing. She ceased resisting him physically. She was hopelessly outmatched by his superior physical strength. She would only survive by her wits. And she was genuinely curious. "What happened?"

He raked fingers through his mussed hair. "That son of a bitch Skye. He tried to kill me! He pushed me off a cliff, into a damn herd of stampeding cattle!"

She bit her lips and refrained from smiling. Skye had not forgotten about her!

"Thank goodness you survived," she said.

"Yeah, right. You're in cahoots with him, you jezebel."

"No, Cal, that's not true!" The protestation didn't sound convincing even to her ears.

"Where were you fixing to ride off to?" he asked. "You've got yourself a horse ready for travel. You tell me the truth now."

"I was going to ride out to see if I could find you," she said. "I wanted to help."

He gave a harsh twist to her wrist. She cried out as he applied excruciating pressure, stopping just short of snapping the joint.

"The truth I said, damn your eyes!" His voice, like his appearance, was ragged, strained. "Where is that bastard? You know. Tell me!" He released some pressure but did not let her go. "What do you know?"

"Nothing! I swear! Really, Cal. Truly. I saw him for the first time yesterday when I was with you, when he rode in and said he was looking for a job. You remember."

"And you haven't seen spoken to him since?"

"I swear I haven't."

Taggart tottered but remained standing. "Everything I've built up," he bellowed, the words slurred, "turning to nothing overnight. It started when that buckskinned bastard showed up."

She looked down, drawing attention to where he held her wrist. "Cal, please. Let go of me. You know I can't get away. Tell me what happened. I want to know."

He considered this and released her. She stepped back, massaging her chafed wrist.

"I don't know how the devil I survived." He muttered more in recollection to himself rather than speaking to her. "It was a stampede. I went over the edge of a drop-off. But when I landed, the herd had mostly passed by and there were only some strays left to stomp me, trying to catch up with the herd." He winced. "They did a pretty good number on me at that. There was dust everywhere, so I don't know if he even saw what happened to me after I went over. I think I busted a rib, and a steer banged up my head bad so I was out for a while. When I came to, the dust had settled. There were dead men everywhere, my men and Yates's hands, too, dead or dying. I got me one of their horses."

"I didn't hear you ride up."

He snickered. "I didn't ride up. I left the horse a ways from here. I wanted to come in quiet and see what you're up to with your friend."

"Cal, I swear I don't know him."

"You've met him though." Jealousy roused Taggart. He drew himself erect. "He was prowling here last night. He came for you. Don't deny it."

She cast her eyes downward. "I won't deny it. But I'm telling the truth. I don't know him."

Taggart snarled, satisfied. "Well, you were smart not to go with him last night. And you'd better not be fixing to double-cross me tonight." He unholstered the revolver at his side. "Where is he, dammit? He thinks I'm dead, doesn't he?"

"Cal, I don't know what he thinks! I tell you, I don't know where he is! I don't know *who* he is!"

Horsemen approaching at a gallop caused them both to turn where they stood in the stable entrance.

Three horsemen rode into the yard, their features obscured by the night. They did not hail the ranch as was customary.

Fear etched itself into Taggart's savagery. "Here he comes now." He waggled the revolver he held at his side. "If anything goes wrong, you treacherous bitch, you'll be the first to die."

The horsemen drew up. Two of them held back, and Britt could hardly see them in the glow.

She paid no attention to them. Her attention was on the man who reined his horse forward.

"Hello, Mr. Mandell."

She did not recognize her own voice. At first, her heartbeat had risen. She'd thought Taggart was right, that Skye was leading men to her rescue! But with recognition of this man atop the horse, staring down at her and Taggart, she didn't know what to think.

Taggart faced Mandell with the revolver at his side. "So," he sneered, "you're mister moneybags."

"That's right." Mandell wore a duster of stylish cut. He presented a commanding image atop his horse. "I am the man you and your ruffian friend, Linder, hoodwinked." He addressed Taggart without emotion. "I thought I had this situation well under control. I retained an agent to act on my behalf. Now I wonder."

That would be Skye, thought Britt.

Taggart wavered on his feet, but managed to express belligerence. "What now, moneybags? You're trespassing on my ranch. Your money's been spent, and your woman's been screwed. What are you going to do, tell me to drop my gun?"

"Frankly, sir," said Mandell dispassionately, "I hardly care whether you die holding your gun or not."

A shrug of his shoulders, and the folds of his duster shifted and a sawed-off shotgun seemed to magically materialize in his hands.

The shotgun boomed, amazingly loud, making Britt wince and start involuntarily.

Twin clusters of buckshot blew away much of Taggart's chest, pasting him to a wall in standing position before he pitched onto his face, his back a pulpy horror that glistened blackly in the faint light.

Britt's stomach cramped with nausea. She averted her eyes. She stared at Mandell and tried to speak. She failed. She swallowed, tried again and said, "Please, sir, give me a chance."

Astride his horse, a handsome mare, Mandell broke open the smoking shotgun with a studied casualness. He reloaded, then snapped the shotgun shut, ready to fire again. He looked down at her.

"Hell, you fine young thing, I aim to give you plenty of chances to do all kinds of things." He chortled lewdly. "You'll do what I tell you to do in our bedroom when you're my wife, and in every other room of the house. You understand? I paid for you and I aim to get my money's worth, once that high society trash in Silver City gives you the nod of approval. Then I can go on being an upstanding gentleman and make more money because I'll have a good-looking wife on my arm, all nice and civilized. But between you and me, sister, you do as you're told or I'll have you humping for pesos in one of my houses in Cruces before the month's over, and high society will think you had to go back East to take care of your sick mama." Another shrug and Mandell's shotgun disappeared, returning to beneath the folds of his duster. "Now, have I made myself clear?"

She mumbled, "Yes, sir."

"I didn't hear you, girl."

"I said, yes, sir."

He gave a snort of satisfaction. "That's better. Now mount up. We're heading out."

She sensed a weak point. Not quite certain why, she felt emboldened enough to push it. "Why the hurry, G.B.?"

"Make that sir." He bristled. "No hurry. I just don't care to tangle with that son of a bitch after I paid him to bring you back."

This arrested her attention more than anything did.

"You hired him?"

"Of course he worked for me. Did you think he was some sort of gallant knight come to rescue the damsel in distress? His name is Skye Fargo. And he is a wild card. I'd sure like to know where he is right now."

Shadows shifted.

Britt realized that a man stood next to her, facing Mandell.

It was Fargo, his feet squarely planted, a hand on his holstered Colt.

"I'm right here, Mr. Mandell. What did you have in mind?"

20

It was that time, just after dusk, when night has fallen yet eyes that have adjusted with the coming of darkness can still see.

Figures were discernible. The riders Mandell had brought with him were inky smudges, holding back.

Mandell's shadowy features exhibited no surprise. "Well, well. I reckon you were on the job after all, Mr. Fargo. I stand corrected."

"I reckon you do."

Britt stood next to Fargo, eyeing him. "But how did you get here? How long have you been listening? How much do you know?"

"Taggart wasn't the only one who wanted to size things up," said Fargo. "It's a prudent thing to do. I slipped in through the back of the stable while Mr. Mandell was busy shooting Taggart." He spoke to the man on horseback. "There's the matter of a retainer, payment for me finding your mail-order bride." He nodded to Britt.

"Skye." A frown touched Britt's voice. "Do you mean it was all business?"

Fargo didn't take his eyes from Mandell. "Yeah, honey. You seem like a nice girl, and I always have been fond of you impulsive types. But the only reason I'm here is because your intended, that would be Mr. Mandell, hired me to track you down and bring you home."

"I see," she said in a small voice.

Mandell cleared his throat. "I hope you don't mind

me drawing your attention, sir, to the fact that I did arrive here to locate Miss Lundgren before your arrival. That renders payment of the second half of your retainer null and void."

"How did you track her down?" asked Fargo. "My guess would be that fella and his daughter at the stage station."

Britt gasped. "You didn't harm them, did you?" she demanded of Mandell.

"No reason to," said Mandell expansively. "I'm not a bad man. I just want to keep hold of what's mine and use it to get more. In this case, miss, I am talking about you."

Fargo said, "Yeah, let's talk about her. But first, let's me and you talk about that retainer."

"You dispute my assessment of the situation?" Mandell nodded at the inky forms of the riders. "These men are heavily armed with weapons that they know how to use. You don't stand a chance, Fargo. Don't try to get any more money out of me."

Fargo laughed. "Mister, have you got me wrong. I don't want more money from you. Hell, I'll give you back the first half of that retainer you paid me."

"Say again," said Mandell.

"I said, I don't want your money."

"Well, I declare." Mandell chuckled. "You don't want my money? That's a new one on me, mister. Never heard anyone say that to me before, no sir."

"Skye," Britt said softly, a whisper like a breeze, "what are you saying?"

"I'm saying that it's not right for one person to act like they own another because some money changed hands, like in this mail-order bride business. Mr. Mandell, this woman is free to do whatever she wants without you tracking her down like she's your property."

"I see," said Mandell. "How noble. And I suppose you're going to return my money and tell me that all prior agreements are off. You intend to escort the lady out of here, is that it?"

"Yes, sir, that's it. The money you paid me is still in my pocket."

"Well, the plain and simple truth of the matter is, it's not going to happen like that," said Mandell. "Fact is, this filly does belong to me and I'll kill anyone who says different. I could have you shot like a dog right now, Fargo, and take my money off of your useless carcass after you're dead."

Britt whispered, "Be careful, Skye. He's got a shotgun under his duster."

"I know, kitten. Back off. Find cover." He sensed more than saw the movement to his side as Britt shuffled into deeper darkness. Then he was addressing the man on horseback. "I'm a tricky bastard, Mandell."

Mandell chuckled. "I know. I like the way you played those two big shots off each other, to pluck my girl out of it. That was real good."

"Good enough to get me killed?"

"I told you," said Mandell. "You're dead because you stand in the way of me taking my woman home."

"I'm a tricky bastard," said Fargo, "and you're a cheap bastard. Chew on this, Mandell. What if I just told you a lie, since I'm so damn clever? What if the money you paid me isn't on me, but I can tell you where it is? Are you going to shoot me right off and risk losing that chunk of cash? You'll want to search me first to make sure I've got your money, then kill me. What the hell kind of businessman are you?"

"You bastard," said Mandell. He left the saddle, coming furiously at Fargo, starting to bring up the shotgun. "I'll cut you to ribbons. Give me my damn money."

"Not tonight," said Fargo.

The looming shadows in the yard outside moved, and he had the impression that the riders were nudging their horses in closer. The black descent of night made it more and more difficult to see.

Fargo used this as cover to step in close before Mandell could bring the shotgun up from the folds of his duster. He tore the shotgun from Mandell's grip and tossed it aside. In the same motion, he brought Mandell around and yanked the duster down around Mandell's arms, stymieing his movement.

Mandell had time only for a surprised gasp. "What the hell?" Fargo took him by the back, like a barman giving a drunk the bum's rush, and it dawned on Mandell what was happening. "No!" he shouted. *"No!"*

Fargo shoved him into the darkness beyond the entrance. He drew his revolver and fired twice at where Mandell's riders would be, then flung himself to the earthen floor of the stable, beneath a blistering volley of return fire that flared the night and raked the entranceway with bullets.

Mandell had no time to cry out, still stumbling from Fargo's shove when first one heavy slug, then another, then another cored through his upper body, making him a stumbling dead man. He dropped.

Silence.

The yard seemed even darker after the flaring muzzle flashes. Gunsmoke drifted on the air.

Fargo had his Colt out and up. He darted to the deep shadows where Britt cowered. He crouched, ready for anything, and she ceased to cower after he reached her, standing between her and those in the darkness.

"Mr. Mandell?" one of the horsemen called, a disembodied voice from the black void.

"Mr. Mandell," echoed the other. "Are you all right, sir?"

"He's as *not* all right as a feller can be," called Fargo. "You killed him."

A pause.

"We *what*?"

The other disembodied voice said, "Are you Skye Fargo?"

"I am." He could have fired, could have picked them off easily from the sound of their voices. But he continued to hope that the killing would stop.

"And, uh, Mr. Mandell, he's really dead?"

"You boys killed him just now," Fargo said in a conversational tone. "I don't know what he told you to get you to sign onto this fandango, but whatever he paid you, it ain't worth dying for."

Another pause. They considered.

The first disembodied voice called, "Are you willing to let us ride off, free and clear?"

"You haven't done me any harm," said Fargo. "I look at it this way. None of us has a stake in this, now that Mandell is dead. You boys take what you were paid and ride off, the both of you."

"Mr. Fargo, you prove yourself to be a gentleman of integrity and damn good ideas."

The other added, "Much obliged."

There came the sounds of the riders wheeling their mounts about and galloping from the yard. The hoofbeats receded into the night, diminishing to nothing. There was only the night breeze through the rafters of the stable; the rich, earthy, natural, not unpleasant smell of the stable; the whinny of Britt's saddled horse farther back in the gloom of the stable's interior. There was the sound of night insects and the call of a night bird, and another's reply.

The woman joined Fargo in the entrance of the stable. She sidled up close enough to him for their hips to touch, and the natural scent of her tantalized his nostrils, awakening arousal within him. He holstered his Colt, and it seemed the most natural thing in the world to slide his arm around her waist.

She was staring off in the direction taken by the riders. "Do you think they're gone or just playing a trick? Will they circle back?"

"They're lighting out. A dead boss is a good incentive to quit a job in their line of work."

"What will you do? I liked the way you spoke to Mandell about ownership and money. You are a man of honor."

"There was some rough scrapping and no mistake," Fargo considered aloud, "but I didn't have to kill Taggart, Yates, or Mandell. That was taken care of for me by others, and I did get to lend you a hand." He patted his breast pocket, where he carried his folding money. "And I did earn what Mandell paid me, considering that he tried to kill me with a shotgun." He glanced in her direction. "You did a good job of holding up through

172

everything you've been through. And you never had to marry Mandell after all." He gave her a hug. "I guess that makes you free as a bird."

"Free as a bird," she said. "I am still learning your American sayings, you see. Yes, I like that one very much, for it is how I feel. I am as free as a bird." She returned his hug. "You risked your life for me, more than once. You brought down the empires of Yates and Taggart in twenty-four hours. You have given the people of this valley hope for a new life, a new beginning. And you saved me. If it weren't for you, I would be a slave to either Mandell or Taggart. I would not be as free as a bird."

"What happens to you now, free bird?"

"I was about to ride away from here," she said. "I was thinking only that far, you see. I don't know where my next adventure awaits." She turned in his arm to face him. "Or perhaps I do."

Moonrise was hours away. The night could not be more black, illuminated only by starlight. Mandell's body, in the yard where his men had mowed him down, could not be seen. Taggart's body likewise was separated from where they stood by a walled enclosure. It was as if the violence had never happened, and he was alone with this beauty who was clearly offering herself to him. He thought of the women he'd encountered over the past forty-eight hours, from the restless little sodbuster's wife turned honky-tonk girl in Quartz, to sweet Hilde with her fleshy curves and a backbone of steel. He thought of the passionate encounters with Lacy Jay, and the wonderfully exuberant Annie Mae, who sure knew how to cook, despite her lack of prowess in food preparation. But none of them, special as each was, held a candle to the stunning, breathtaking beauty of this blonde who now rested the palms of her hands against his chest, lightly yet surprising him with heat.

"And you, Mr. Skye? Or should I call you Mr. Fargo?"

He tightened his hold of her waist, drawing her closer to him. "You can call me Skye or you can call me Fargo or you can call me darlin', darlin'."

173

"Very well, Skye," she said in that tender, come-hither tone that women, he had come to learn, will use when they've got a man in their sights and know it's only a matter of reeling him in. "What is your next adventure going to be?"

He chuckled. "I think I'm holding her in my arms."

"Is that so?" Her chuckle was like warm, rippling water. "Mighty sure of yourself, aren't you, Buckskin?"

"Well then, let's see," he said, in a mock serious tone. "Before I got sidetracked into this shindig, I was heading to the high country where the nights are cool and a body can use a body to help stay warm."

"That sounds inviting."

"So do you," he ventured. He slipped his other arm around her. She was leggy, muscular, high-breasted, firm-hipped. "You're welcome to ride with me as long as that restless nature of yours has a mind to," he said, "or for as long as we can put up with each other, whichever comes first."

She stood on her tiptoes so that her pelvis glided pleasantly against his hardening shaft. Her shapely breasts pressed against his chest, her nipples erect. Her hands encircled his neck and drew him down so that her lips fluttered against his ear like a butterfly's wings, hot breath whispering.

"And you're welcome to ride me right here, right now, Skye Fargo. Don't you think we deserve it?" Her tongue flicked, wet and darting.

"Yeah, now that you mention it," said Fargo, "I reckon we do."

And they fell into the hay together.

LOOKING FORWARD!
The following is the opening
section from the next novel in the exciting
Trailsman series from Signet:

THE TRAILSMAN #251
Utah Uproar

The Great Salt Lake Desert, 1861—
unexplored, unrelenting, and certain
death for the unwary.

The tall man in buckskins was about seventy-five miles
west of Salt Lake City when a whirlwind of death roared
down on him.

Skye Fargo had left Salt Lake several days before,
bound for California. It was the middle of the summer
and daytime temperatures were well over one hundred
degrees. As a result, he traveled at night rather than
during the day to spare his pinto stallion from being
roasted alive. Now, well out into the Great Salt Lake
Desert, Fargo felt a sudden gust of wind on his bearded
face. His piercing lake-blue eyes scanned the star-
sprinkled heavens to the west, seeking sign of an approaching storm. But the sky was crystal clear, the night
serene. Not even a single star was blotted out by clouds.

Fargo had been following a rutted track that wound across the desert. In a couple more days he would reach the small settlement of Wendover. Until then, he had to be on his guard against roving bands of hostile Utes. The tribe was at odds with the Mormons over the loss of land. Not all that long ago a bitter war had been fought, and while a truce was supposedly in effect, a number of whites had disappeared without a trace.

Fargo also had to be on his watch against the elements. Thunderstorms were common this time of year. For a rider to be caught in the open in one was as dangerous as being caught by a Ute war party; flash floods and lightning had claimed many a life. So when another gust of wind buffeted him, Fargo became concerned. It was much too strong for a typical breeze. He sniffed the air but detected no trace of moisture, as there would be if a storm front were approaching.

That left one possibility.

Every nerve taut, Fargo rode on. He hoped he was wrong. He hoped there wouldn't be any more gusts of wind. But he hadn't gone another fifty yards when the strongest one yet buffeted him, nearly taking his hat off.

"I don't like this, fella," Fargo said aloud to the Ovaro as he jammed his hat back down onto his head. He had a habit of talking to the pinto during long, lonely stretches on the trail. The stallion snorted, as if in agreement, and pricked up its ears as if it had caught a faint sound.

Fargo listened but heard nothing. He sniffed the night air again but smelled nothing. He tried to convince himself he was making too much out of it. That all would be well. That the stallion must have heard a coyote or a mountain lion.

Then the wind returned with a vengeance, a ferocious blast that nearly took Fargo's breath away and whipped the fringe on his buckskins. A few stinging grains of sand pelted him, harbingers of much worse to come.

"Sandstorm!" Fargo breathed. They had to find a spot

to take shelter. He surveyed the flat, bleak landscape but all he saw were a few scattered boulders. To the north and west lay more of the same. To the south, though, was an isolated mountain range rarely visited by either whites or red man. There were plenty of places to wait out Nature's temper tantrum in relative safety. A prick of his spurs galvanized the pinto into a trot, but he doubted the windstorm would hold off long enough for them to get there. Unfortunately, he was right.

Fargo had barely gone a mile when the wind doubled in intensity. Fine particles of sand pelted every exposed inch of his skin. He had to squint to keep it from getting into his eyes. In the distance wind-spawned shrieks keened like a chorus of the damned unleashed from the pit of hell.

The Ovaro gamely trotted on, seemingly impervious to the barrage of sand. But Fargo knew better. Drawing rein, he dismounted, hastily opened a saddlebag, and took out his spare shirt. He stepped in front of the stallion and raised it to tie it over the Ovaro's eyes to shield them. But just as he did, an especially powerful blast of screaming wind tore it from his grasp and flung the flapping garment against the Ovaro. The horse did what most any other would do; whinnying in fright, it shied and pranced wildly away.

"No!" Fargo hollered. He lunged to grab hold of the reins but his fingers closed on thin air.

The Ovaro was in full flight, the shirt still partially wrapped around its head and upper neck, the shirt sleeves flapping wildly.

Fargo ran after it. A useless gesture, since within moments his horse had melted into the murk. He drew up short, staggered by the cruel trick fate had played. To be stranded afoot was bad enough. To be stranded with a sandstorm about to break in all its raging elemental might was a calamity. Not only for him, but also for the stallion. Left on its own, exposed and unprotected, the Ovaro might very well die.

Nearby was a waist-high boulder. Not much cover, but enough that if Fargo were to curl up into a ball at its base and covered his head with both arms, he could wait out the worst of the ordeal to come. But if he did, he gave up any hope of recovering the Ovaro. He doggedly ran on.

The wind pummeled him with invisible fists. The sand stung like a swarm of angry bees. And all the while the shrieking grew louder. It wouldn't be long now. The sandstorm was almost on top of him. Fargo's boots sent up fine plumes of the whitish sand with every stride, plumes instantly blown apart like so many wisps of smoke.

Unbidden, Fargo remembered the time he came on a pair of skeletons in an Arizona desert. A prospector and a mule had been caught in a sandstorm and sought haven on the lee side of a dune. They ended up buried alive. If a freak rainstorm hadn't later washed away part of the dune shortly before he happened by, no one would ever have known.

Then there was the Brockman party, a wagon train bound for the promised land of Oregon. Eleven families had been caught far from anywhere when a sandstorm descended upon them. An army patrol found the survivors. All four of them. Their wagons were in ruins, most upended, the canvas tops ripped to ribbons. And every last animal had either run off, never to be seen again, or perished outright.

Fargo gave a toss of his head, derailing his train of thought. There were also people who had lived through sandstorms and he intended to be one of them. But first he had to find the Ovaro. He kept hoping the pinto hadn't run that far. At any moment he might stumble across it.

Visibility had been reduced to twenty feet and was lessening rapidly. One arm in front of his eyes, Fargo shouted, "Here, boy! Over here, big fella!" But his cry was smothered by the wind.

How far Fargo ran, he couldn't say. Maybe a mile. Maybe two. Suddenly the sky was rent by a titanic howl of unearthly proportions and the sandstorm swooped down in all its terrible might, engulfing the desert in a cyclonic gale that had to be experienced to be believed.

In the blink of an eye, Fargo couldn't see any further than the end of his arm. So much sand was in the air, it hurt to breathe. It got into his nose and filled his mouth. His eyes were mercilessly battered and wouldn't stop watering. Pressing both forearms over his face, he stumbled on, half-blinded, barely able to catch a decent breath. He needed to stop and dig in. *But where?* He cast about for a boulder, a gully, any place that would afford some small measure of protection. But there was none.

To complicate matters, Fargo had lost all sense of direction. Without the stars to guide him, he wasn't sure if he was still heading south. He might be traveling east or west. Slowing, he peered hard into the swirling tempest, desperate to find cover. But his eyes were so irritated by all of the sand that had gotten into them, the world around him was a watery blur.

"Damn!" Fargo swore aloud, and promptly regretted it when a fistful of sand was blown halfway down his throat. He tried to spit it out, but in opening his mouth he admitted more. Gagging, he doubled over. He spit out as much of the sand as he could, but his mouth and throat were still layered with it.

Without warning, a wall of wind slammed into him, nearly blowing Fargo over. It started to tear his hat off. He clutched at the brim but was too slow. The hat went sailing off into the storm.

Fargo lurched forward, groping blindly. He had to keep his eyes nearly shut. Not that they were of much use anyway. His right boot scraped a boulder and he bent low to gauge the size. It didn't come any higher than the middle of his shins and wouldn't afford the haven he needed. Struggling to keep his balance against the pummeling wind, he trudged on.

Although folks said he was as strong as bull, Fargo had his limits. This relentless onslaught of the wind, this ceaseless bombardment of sand, were more than any man could endure indefinitely. His strength and his energy were swiftly being sapped. Then his left boot bumped something in his path. His questing fingers found a cluster of large boulders. Carefully easing in among them, Fargo sank to his knees and lowered his forehead to the ground. Sand still pelted him, but nowhere near as much. And here he was spared the brunt of the rampaging wind. Wrapping his arms around his head, he resigned himself to being stuck there for a spell.

Fargo couldn't stop thinking about the Ovaro. He had ridden that horse from one end of the country to the other, from the Gulf of Mexico to the Canadian border, from the Mississippi River to the Pacific Ocean. Seldom had it ever let him down. He would sooner part with an arm or a leg, and the thought of the Ovaro out there somewhere, helpless and alone, had him grinding his teeth in frustration.

Around him chaos reigned. Caterwauling like a million wildcats, the wind never slackened. Nor did the blistering onslaught of sand. Fargo could feel it crawl up under his shirt and down into his pants. Without a blanket to cover himself with, he was forced to endure whatever the storm dished out.

Fargo's eyes were on fire, but he resisted an urge to wipe his sleeve against them. It would only aggravate them further. He needed water to do the job properly. Unfortunately, his canteen was on the Ovaro. So were his rifle, his bedroll, and practically every personal article he owned. He chose not to dwell on the consequences should he fail to reclaim them.

The minutes dragged into an eternity. It might have been two hours later, it might have been four, when Fargo realized the banshee wail was tapering off and the tornadic upheaval was dying. He raised his head, wincing at a cramp in his neck, and was startled to discover the gap between the boulders had filled up with sand past his hips. He could barely move his legs. With an effort, he rose onto his knees. The night was an impenetrable curtain of darkness, the sky was obscured. He wouldn't be able to get his bearings until he could see the stars again.

The wind was down to a whisper. Relieved the storm hadn't lasted any longer, Fargo placed his hands flat against a boulder to rise, then paused. From the west wafted a shrill whine. It might be nothing. Then again, it could be that the storm wasn't over, that this was a lull before another blast was unleashed. He listened intently, and sure enough, the whine slowly grew until it resembled the cry of a woman in dire distress.

Fargo bent low just as the sandstorm renewed its assault with magnified ferocity. What had gone before was mild compared to the volcanic eruption that now took place. Within moments Fargo was being scoured by buckets of sand hurled by a whirlwind of titanic proportions. And all he could do was hunker down and bear it.

The level of the sand encasing Fargo steadily rose. It was soon above his belt. At the rate the gap was filling, it wouldn't be long before he ended up sharing the fate of the man who had been buried alive. He pushed at the growing pile to shove as much as he could from between the boulders, but for every handful he dislodged, the wind deposited a gallon to take its place.

Grains were trickling into Fargo's ears and down into his boots. He spat repeatedly but he couldn't get the hard grains out of his mouth.

It was then, at the height of the sandstorm, that Fargo thought he heard a whinny coming from somewhere nearby. Believing it to be the Ovaro, he automatically sat up again, full into the wind. It violently shoved him against a boulder. Inadvertently, he opened his eyes all the way, and was spiked by tiny daggers that threatened to strip his sight away.

Doubling over, Fargo covered his eyes with his hands.

He had no choice but to stay there as long as he could, even at the risk of being buried alive. The Ovaro, he reluctantly conceded, was on its own until it was safe for him to move about.

Inky blackness veiled the world. Fargo peeked between his fingers now and then but saw no sign that the storm was abating. If it didn't stop soon, he would have a decision to make. Should he stay there and be buried or go in search of better sanctuary? It was a case of damned if he did, damned if he didn't. Whichever he chose, the prospects were grim.

Fargo opted to stay put. Out in the open he wouldn't last sixty seconds. His skin would be flayed from his body and his lungs would succumb to the lack of breathable air. A decade down the road someone might stumble across his remains and have the decency to bury them. If not, his bleached skull would serve as a warning to all those who came after.

Fargo went to shift his right arm to relieve a pain in his elbow, and couldn't. The sand had risen to within a hand's width of his shoulders, pinning his arms in place. In a fit of anger he pulled loose, and in so doing more sand got into his nose and mouth. It felt as if he were inhaling shards of glass.

Of the many ways Fargo had imagined dying, this wasn't one of them. Frontiersmen lived notoriously short lives. Each and every day they had to contend with a thousand and one ways of dying. Wild beasts, painted hostiles, Nature's temper tantrums, all of which took a constant toll. Fargo always thought he would die in a gunfight or in a battle with warriors out to lift his scalp, not smothered to death in a sandstorm.

The level continued to rise. It was now just below his chin. Fargo had to get out of there before it was too late. Surging upward, he rose a few inches but couldn't fully straighten. The sand hemmed him like a straightjacket. By twisting back and forth he began to loosen its grip, but in the meantime the storm pounded him without quarter. His face hurt abominably. He dared not do more than crack his eyelids, for to open them wider invited permanent blindness.

With a tremendous wrench, Fargo tore clear and tottered out from among the boulders. He had gone from the proverbial frying pan into the proverbial fire. Out in the open, the full weight of the storm bore down his shoulders. The hammering wind drove him to his knees, the rampant sand cut and stung like a thousand tiny knives.

Willing his legs to work, Fargo staggered forward in search of shelter. He had no idea in which direction he was going. Again and again, he bumped into small boulders, spiking pain up his legs. Several times he tripped, and once he fell to his hands and knees. Deprived of his senses, he was as helpless as an infant. A reminder, as if any were needed, that in the scheme of things man was no more than a flickering flame on a candle, to be extinguished at Nature's whim.

On and on Fargo plodded, but sanctuary was denied him. Gradually his energy was sapped as his great strength ebbed. His legs became wooden, his arms stiff. Each time he swallowed, he swore his throat was being ripped raw. It was like swallowing a cup of tiny glass shards.

Just when it seemed the most hopeless, Fargo was dealt the cruelest card yet. His next step was into empty space. Instinctively, he jerked back, but his legs were swept out from under him and he tumbled end over end. A jarring blow brought his careening plunge to a halt. The darkness deepened and his mind swam in pitch.

Rolling onto his stomach, Fargo got his hands under his chest. He levered upward, only to have his sinews betray him. His cheek smacked the earth. He wanted to rise but couldn't. His last sensation was of the remorseless sand pelting him. His last thought was that this was a damned stupid way to die.

No other series has this much historical action!

THE TRAILSMAN

To order call: 1-800-788-6262